PRAISE FOR *THE RIDDLE OF THE*

The Riddle of the Graveyard *is a fun read and a great example of the magic that can happen when you combine a creative imagination with strong writing and a deep understanding of boats and life on a small island. Bravo, Peter!*

—BILL LYNN, President and Executive Director,
Herreshoff Marine Museum

~~~

The novel brings back wonderful memories of Martha's Vineyard summers and strengthening friendships as teenagers—when our boats and access to the water always promised adventure and exploration (albeit not as exciting or scary as confronting the gang in this book).

—DAVID VIETOR, America's Cup syndicate
vice chairman and helmsman

~~~

Peter Hufstader has written the sort of adventure story I dreamed of having when I was a boy learning to sail. But it's all the more thrilling because it asks young people to imagine how they would have coped on menacing near-shore waters in a world before GPS, Doppler radar, and cell phones. Just you, your skills, and your ability to out-think and out-sail your grown-up antagonists—man, what could be better than that!

—TOM DUNLOP, author
Schooner: Building a Wooden Boat on Martha's Vineyard

The Riddle
of the Graveyard

The Riddle
of the Graveyard

Peter Hufstader

Hedge Fence Press

Thank you to Elizabeth Balay for images on pages 169, 170, 172, 175, 177.
To Christopher Cunningham for image page 173.

Library of Congress Number: 2018934485

ISBN: 978-0-692-07280-6

Book design: Jill Dible, Atlanta, GA
Cover illustration: Lane Gregory, Martha's Vineyard, MA
Printed in the United States

For my Grandchildren
Nick and Kit Balay
and
Lucy and Charlie Moore

CONTENTS

Miguel's Dream 11

Crime Comes to Old Town 13

The Golden Crucifix 21

Phoenix Meets *Thresher* 29

The Authorities Take Charge 33

"You Can't Go Near the Graveyard" 38

Chart 471 43

The Lane through the Graveyard 48

The Meaning of Miguel's Dream 56

Cap'n Ben Hears a Story 69

The Passage to Quarantine Island 73

Quarantine Island 76

Going It Alone 88

Rendezvous at the Bend 94

Twin Decisions 102

Prisoners Aboard *Thresher* 107

Rescue 112

The Battle with the Sea Skiff 122

Schoodic Head Finds *Loon* 135

Sailors Home 138

The Reckoning 148

Looking Ahead 155

Loose Ends 159

Author's Note 165

Glossary 166

Miguel's Dream

Midnight, Wednesday, August 30

The boy sleeping on the rumpled bed suddenly gasped, started up on one elbow, and froze, his head cocked toward the open window.

The boy listened a long moment to the muslin curtains whispering gently across the window shades in the moist night air. Then he slowly exhaled, sat up, and freed his legs from the tangled sheets. Kneeling in front of the open window, he pushed the whispering curtains to either side and rested his arms on the sill.

There was no moon. The stars had vanished. Miguel could just make out the pale edge of the beach beyond the dark mass of dunes. That ghostly blob floating offshore must be *Loon*'s white hull. He searched for *Phoenix*, but the night had swallowed the green-hulled dory.

Miguel listened a few more minutes, inhaling the briny tang of Shellfish Bay, but he heard only the harsh *quawk* of a night heron. He turned slightly to his left. The house next door was dark. The twins were asleep.

Miguel drew the white curtains across the window and sat back on his bed. He glanced at his bureau. For a moment he thought his brand-new clock had lost a hand. Then he realized it was midnight.

Miguel yawned and lay back on his pillow.

Musta been a dream. Nothin's buzzin' out there.

~~~

As Miguel sank back to sleep, a white shape emerged from the darkness and drifted silently toward the beach below his house. A boat grounded with a faint, sliding crunch.

For several moments nothing moved. Then a dark figure slithered over the boat's bow, glided across the pale beach toward the shadowy dunes, and vanished.

Miguel was sound asleep, his covers thrown back and his face turned away from the open window, when a humpbacked figure detached itself from the shadow of the dunes and lumbered toward the boat.

Before the figure reached the water's edge, it stopped and crouched. Miguel heard neither the faint *chink* nor the muffled grunts that followed. He was sleeping deeply when the boat slid off the beach and vanished into the gloom. Then there was only silence.

Minutes later, somewhere out in the darkness of Shellfish Bay, a light engine coughed, caught, then steadied to a gentle buzz that faded, faded, and died.

Once again the only sound was the papery whispering of the muslin curtains wafting back and forth, back and forth, across the window shades.

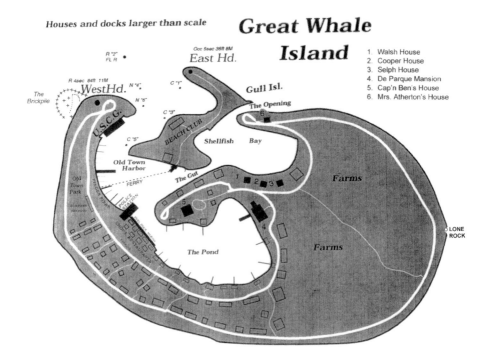

Houses and docks larger than scale

Great Whale Island

East Hd.

Gull Isl.

WestHd.

The Brickpile

U.S.C.G.

BEACH CLUB

Shellfish Bay

The Opening

Old Town Harbor

Old Town Park

FERRY

POLICE STATION

The Gut

The Pond

Farms

Farms

LONE ROCK

1. Walsh House
2. Cooper House
3. Selph House
4. De Parque Mansion
5. Cap'n Ben's House
6. Mrs. Atherton's House

Crime Comes to Old Town

Thursday Morning, August 31

Betty Cooper pushed the toaster's plunger, then turned to watch her fifteen-year-old twins blinking themselves awake.

Jon, dressed in smelly work jeans and knee-high rubber boots, his chambray work shirt misbuttoned, was gulping coffee between cadaverous yawns while Abbie, still in her panda pajamas, rooted irritably in the roundabout cupboard.

"Jon, did you eat up all the Snappy Pops again?"

"They're on the table, Abbie," Betty Cooper said quickly. "What time's Ferdie picking you up, Jonno?"

"Seven." Jon looked at the clock over the old black stove. It was 6:55. The toaster gave its familiar "sprang!" Two brown semicircles shot into view and sat quivering in their slots. Jon snatched the English muffin halves with his fingertips, dropped them hastily on a plate, and reached for the jar of peanut butter.

Abbie placed her cereal bowl and spoon neatly on a place mat and pulled out her chair. "Where's Dad?" she asked the Snappy Pops.

"Sergeant Maciel called a little after six." Betty Cooper looked down at her daughter's tousled blond head. "Dad said I could tell you."

Abbie looked up, her spoon halfway to her mouth.

"There's been a burglary."

Abbie put her spoon down. "A burglary!"

"Burglary!" Jon echoed, his freckled face astonished. "Who got burglared?"

"The de Parques got burgled."

"The poor de Parques!" Abbie's round face was indignant.

"Yes," her mother said. "They are very nice people. And very rich. I guess someone knew that."

"What got stolen?"

"Dad didn't tell me. He just whistled when Vernon told him."

Ow-OOO-ga! Ow-OOO-ga!

Hearing the horn, Jon jammed the second English muffin between his teeth and snatched his yellow oilskins from their hook.

"We could use four pound-and-a-halfs for dinner!" Betty Cooper called after him, smiling at the muffin-muffled response. A door slammed. Betty Cooper heard Ferdie's Model A pickup groan away from the curb and rattle off down Water Street.

~~~

Old Town was coming to life as Jon and Ferdie bounced over Lower Water Street's cobbles. They waved at Mr. Herbert the green grocer stacking carrots and potatoes on wooden stands in front of his shop, then at Peter Coffin the pharmacist, just rolling out the awnings to keep the sun from striking the huge vermilion and emerald carboys in his store window.

On they rattled, past the dry goods store where Jon got his yellow oilskins ($2 for the top, $2.25 for the pants), past the redbrick Old Town National Bank (Est. 1834), past the Great Whale Island Historical Society, past the gay little boutiques that fronted the harbor, past Bosun, the harbormaster's enormous Newfoundland retriever, chained outside his master's shack near the Town Dock. Bosun liked to "rescue" swimmers at the town's beaches.

"Hey, Bosun!"

Bosun raised his massive head and "whuffed" as his friends rattled past.

Lastly they waved to old Benny standing in the door of his chandlery just south of the shipyard, a dark old shop filled with coils of cotton line, hemp line, and wire. Wooden pegs fixed in the walls held balls of tarry Italian marline. Wooden cheek blocks dangled from the rafters. The floor was clogged with stacked wooden boxes filled with chain, thimbles, bronze cleats, turnbuckles, and shackles.

Jon especially loved the old-fashioned box compasses Benny still stocked, their cards showing the traditional points of the compass rather than the newer cards marked off in degrees. The box compass the twins had been given for their thirteenth birthday had been aboard *Loon* ever since. Sara and Miguel had one aboard *Phoenix*.

Benny's chandlery was the last remnant of the major New England whaling port Old Town had been before the discovery of petroleum in 1859. The relics of the whaling era now repose in the Old Town Historical Society: ancient daguerreotypes of black-coated captains and their grim-looking wives clad from neck to ankle in black and gray, ebony canes with beautifully carved scrimshaw knobs, leather-and-canvas log books, primitive oil paintings, letters whale men wrote home during their four-year-long voyages, letters from wives and children carried by outbound whalers to ports where voyagers might call.

One hundred years ago, Jon knew, the gray-shingled buildings that now housed chic little boutiques had been shops where Old Town's coopers made the barrels that held oil rendered from whale blubber. One hundred years ago the boutique they were just rattling by, its windows filled with sightless mannequins draped in flowery pastel dresses, had been a cooperage owned by Ezred Cooper, Jon's great-great-grandfather, whose daguerreotyped image hangs in the Historical Society's "Whaling Days" exhibit. Jon's father always maintained that Ezred's last name and his occupation were coincidences.

Old Town's cooperages, its sailmakers' lofts, and its ropewalk had vanished. The cedar-scented wood-framed building that had once turned out whaleboats was now an art gallery. The roaring foundry that had forged the iron implements whale ships depended on—cask hoops, harpoon heads, lance heads, massive hoisting hooks for burton tackles, sheaves for turning blocks, eye-bolts, chain—had dwindled to a blacksmith's forge, which had finally yielded to a bicycle shop.

Old Town's sturdy whale ships—*Mercury, Galatea, Sachem, Azro P. Coffin, Ockmulgee, Prudence*—had been replaced by big spoon-bow schooners that fished for cod on the Grand Banks. After the Great War the sailing schooners had been converted to engine-driven draggers and trawlers, their towering topmasts gone, their lower masts now stumps. The only canvas left aboard these former queens of the Grand Banks were dingy little steadying sails.

Descendants of the Azoreans who had sailed as seamen and boat-steerers aboard Old Town's whale ships now fished for lobster or cod, as Ferdie Bettencourt did, or they were tradesmen depending on summer residents and tourists to tide them over the winter.

Ferdie backed the pickup into its slot in front of the row of fishermen's shacks that lined Old Town's working waterfront just south of the fish market, the gas dock, and the Coast Guard Station. While Ferdie rummaged in his shack, Jon clambered aboard *Rosie*, a high-bowed Nova Scotia lobsterman, and took the lid off the spudge barrel*, gagging as he peered inside.

Last time this summer I have to do that, he thought. Tomorrow Ferdie and "the Missus" were taking *Rosie* over to Mackerel Port on Orca Island to spend the holiday weekend with a married daughter and the grandchildren.

When Ferdie emerged from the boat shack, he would fire up *Rosie*'s engine. Jon would take in the bow and stern lines and stand by the after spring line. When Ferdie nodded, Jon would snake the spring line aboard. The engine would change pitch as Ferdie shoved the long gear lever sticking up through the engine hatch to its forward position and advanced the quadrant throttle. Then *Rosie* would move slowly out of her finger pier, turn into the main channel, and head for the fish market to pick up more rotting fish heads—lobsters' favorite food. Then over to the gas dock to top up *Rosie*'s tanks. There was plenty of gas now, five years after the end of World War II, though Ferdie deeply resented having to pay twenty-five cents a gallon for it.

The end of the war had changed Great Whale Island. Less than a year later, people from the mainland started buying up the nineteenth-century Greek Revival mansions built by Old Town's whale ship owners. Almost overnight Old Town became a summer playground for mainland families. They soon bought the wharf where the whalers and the Grand Bankers had refitted between voyages. There the newcomers

---

* See the Glossary for definitions of this and other terms.

established the exclusive Old Town Sailing Club. The sign on its gate read "Members and Guests Only."

When they were out in *Loon* and *Phoenix*, the Cooper twins and the Selphs would sometimes wave to the summer kids in their racing dinghies. Earlier in the summer, when all four friends were sailing in *Loon*, they had played sponge tag with a few of the fast little dinghies. The gaff-rigged *Loon* had been hopelessly outmaneuvered, but it was fun—and very wet.

Fun or not, Jon knew that neither he nor Abbie nor their best friend, Sara, nor her little brother, Miguel, could sail in the sailing club's races. They weren't wanted as "Guests."

Some summer evenings, when the breeze wafting across the harbor was westerly, the Selphs and the Coopers could hear dance music.

No getting around it: the island kids and the summer visitors lived in different worlds. None of the summer kids smelled of rotten fish heads as Jon did after a trip with Ferdie. Some of the summer kids even had their own cars—the latest postwar models!

Most Great Whale Island vehicles were carefully tended Depression-era Model A Fords, like Ferdie's pickup. Earlier that summer, the Old Town Police Department had bought a new cruiser, the first postwar car ever to live year-round on the island—and it had been bought used.

Well, anyway. Monday was Labor Day. Most of the summer people had already left for the mainland and whatever life they lived there. The Coopers and the Selphs stayed.

~~~

Abbie looked out the window at the de Parques' redbrick chimneys soaring above the oaks and elms on the far side of Water Street. *How do burglars get into your house? What if you're there when they break in?*

"Mom?"

"Yes, Sweetie?" Betty Cooper said absently, making a note in the Old Town Hardware Store's ledger.

"Do we have keys?"

Abbie's mother looked up.

"To lock the house?"

Betty Cooper closed the ledger. Abbie was staring out the window across Water Street.

Betty crossed the kitchen and hugged Abbie. "They're around. Somewhere. We've never had to use them before." She smiled. "Maybe we should start now."

Abbie's blue eyes were still troubled. Betty Cooper gave her another hug, then went to a wall cupboard. "You all set for the day, Abbie?"

"All set, Mom. I'm taking the kids to the beach club while Mrs. Walsh packs. They're on the noon ferry tomorrow."

Betty Cooper rummaged in the wall cupboard. "School next week," she said briskly. Abbie groaned.

"I'm *pretty* sure this one fits the back door." Abbie's mother was holding up a bronze skeleton key. "Try it to be sure. Good. You can lock up when you go. But be sure to be home before Dad. He doesn't have a key."

Betty Cooper gathered up her ledgers and account books and stuffed them into a large canvas tote bag. "Okay, I'm off. See you tonight, Abbie. Maybe Jon'll have lobsters for us!"

"See you tonight, Mom."

The screen door banged. Abbie ran to the wall telephone, grabbed the earpiece, and jiggled the hook.

~~~

In the sunny kitchen of the house next door, fifteen-year-old Sara Selph was bent over a book. The kitchen, the family room, Sara's mother working at her desk in the corner, all had vanished. Sara saw only the cold gray walls and damp rooms of Lowood Institution where the orphan girls sickened and died. Miss Temple was just telling Jane, *We shall think you what you prove yourself to be, my child,* when the old wall telephone croaked twice, like a sick frog.

Cold gray walls, Miss Temple's kind voice, Lowood's suffering orphans vanished. Sara shoved back her chair. "I'll get it!" She darted across the kitchen. "Abbie? . . . Oh, hi, Chief Cooper . . . Hang on a second. . . ." Sara put the ear piece on the counter. "Mom, it's Chief Cooper. Where's Dad?"

Marie Selph looked up from a blueprint, her dark eyes smiling. "He just said good-bye to you. Maybe you can catch him."

Sara darted to the back door. "Dad! Dad! Wait! It's Chief Cooper."

Commander Alan Selph, United States Coast Guard, peered around the door jamb. "The chief?"

Sara nodded.

"Morning, Tom . . . Yes, you just caught me. What's up?"

Commander Selph listened intently. "A *what*? . . . I see. . . . That's the. . . ."

Commander Selph listened again. Then he said, "Right. You bet. I'll take quarters and be along at "—he glanced at his wristwatch—"8:30."

The screen door squeaked and slammed.

Sara Selph looked at her mother. "What was *that* all about?"

"I have no idea. Maybe we'll hear about it tonight. Ready for your last day, Sara?"

Sara looked at her new watch. "They're printing the paper now. I can go when we've got the issue folded."

"And tomorrow's your big trip to Sei Island!"

That barren knob of granite, the smallest of the Little Whale Islands, was named for the Sei whale, ironically one of the larger baleen cetaceans. The Norwegian word is pronounced "Say."

Sara rolled her blue eyes. "Finally!" she cried. "We've been waiting all summer! And this is our last weekend!"

Marie Selph's dark eyes studied her daughter. "You know why we waited."

Sara looked down. "Fifteen's plenty old," she said resentfully. "It's only to Sei Island." Sara gestured toward the big bow window. "You can *see* it from here."

Marie Selph knew very well that the purple dome on the horizon was Sei Island. Her eyes didn't leave her daughter. "Fifteen's plenty old if fifteen knows what it's doing and uses good judgment. Whale Sound can be very dangerous. This summer you've had to show us you are competent sailors who make good decisions."

It was like being under a microscope, Sara thought. *Every time something happened they knew about it.*

Marie Selph smiled. "We were pretty worried back in June. Remember when you and Miguel took *Phoenix* over to the gas dock by yourselves?"

"Mom!" Sara protested. But she remembered very well the sickening bang when she ran the little green dory straight into the dock. She had forgotten to tell Miguel, *Phoenix*'s engineer, to put the outboard engine into reverse. Then she had pulled the wrong tiller line.

"Well, that's how you have to learn sometimes. The hard way. And you've gotten pretty good since then. Dad was so proud when you found your way home last week."

"Oh," Sara said offhandedly, as if a pea soup fog was nothing special, "when we saw the fog out in the sound, Jon got a bearing on R '4.' When the fog shut down, we knew exactly where we were and how to get home."

Marie Selph smiled. "That's why Dad was so proud. You were doing what he always says to do. Thinking ahead, preparing for the worst. You know how important that is to us."

Marie Selph's voice changed. "And speaking of important things." Marie Selph waited for Sara's unwilling blue eyes to meet her dark ones. "Remember. You older kids are responsible for Miguel. He's only eleven."

Sara struggled to keep her voice neutral. "I know, Mom. You've told us. We always look out for Miguel."

Marie Selph smiled. Despite herself, Sara smiled back. *How does she do that? Even when I'm mad.*

"The weather's supposed to be beautiful tomorrow," her mother was saying when something thumped loudly against the side of the house. She ran for the back door crying, "Miguel! Miguel!" The screen door squealed and banged shut. Marie Selph's voice faded around the corner of the house. "Miguel! *Stop!*" Another loud thump. "You're going to . . ."

Then Sara heard the familiar crash of breaking glass.

"Miguel! That's the third window this summer!"

The phone croaked again.

The Golden Crucifix

Friday Morning, September 1

G reat Whale Island and the Little Whale Islands were created eons ago when an enormous sheet of ice deposited many billions of tons of ground-up rock and sand as it crunched slowly from what we now call Canada down through New England. Some of this debris eventually formed Cape Halibut, Great Whale Island, and the Little Whale Islands. As the ice sheet melted—it took a mere few thousand years—the water rose, separating the glacier's debris into capes and islands and creating the sounds and bays that wash their shores. Over the millennia, currents and storms battered the glacial deposits into today's sandy coastline and shoals. Currents and storms will continue to hammer these sandy outposts until the sea overwhelms them.

A small-scale chart (*shown on next page*) gives you a good idea of Great Whale Island's shape. Great Whale was still only sparsely populated after World War II, and Old Town was its only settled village. The half-dozen hamlets dotting the island had unofficial names, like Eastville, the collection of cottages huddled near the Opening.

First founded by English settlers in the early seventeenth century, Old Town became one of the most prosperous whaling ports in the world. Great Whale Sound opens directly onto the Atlantic Ocean at both its eastern and western ends, and the Atlantic connects to the other oceans of the world—where the whales were then and are now again. Whether the wind blew from the eastern or the western semicircle, Old Town's whale ships could sail out into Whale Sound and thence directly into the Atlantic.

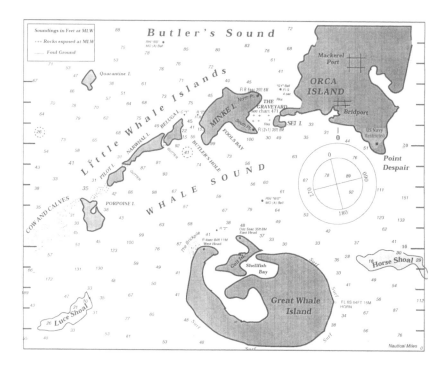

Equally important, the harbor was then and still is superbly protected by Gull Island to the east and by West Head. Once a vessel passes between the two, it is almost as safe as if it were landlocked.

Shellfish Bay, where *Loon* and *Phoenix* were moored from late spring to early fall, is open to Great Whale Sound through a narrow passage called "the Opening" (*depicted on the large-scale chart of Great Whale Island above, as shown*). The Opening can be deadly. When the wind is northerly or easterly, wind-blown waves pushing against a strong ebb tide create breaking seas that can drown the foolhardy—and do so every year. Not only is the Opening dangerous under certain conditions; once you are through it, you are on your own out in the lonely, open waters of Whale Sound.

Loon and *Phoenix* always ran through the Gut, the narrow channel connecting Shellfish Bay to Old Town Harbor. Although the current ran hard through the Gut, especially during each month's spring tides—at the new moon and at the full—there were never any breaking seas in there. And the Gut led to Old Town Harbor, where young boat handlers could practice their skills with help nearby if they needed it.

On this Friday morning, the first of September, the blue waters of Shellfish Bay gleamed like polished metal under the hot morning sun. Urged on by a new moon close to perigee, the flood tide rushed from Whale Sound through the narrow Opening, then swirled along the southern shore of Gull Island and through the narrow Gut that led to Old Town Harbor. There it met the tidal flow pouring between West Head and Gull Island. The mingled currents filled Old Town Harbor and the Pond, the large mooring area south of the harbor.

When the flood tide reached its height, the waters within the encircling arms of Old Town Harbor lay still. Then the moon issued its voiceless commands. The waters in Old Town Harbor, the Pond, and Shellfish Bay moved obediently northward toward Whale Sound and the open ocean. As the tide began to fall, the temperature of the water changed slightly. A southerly wind from the Atlantic Ocean began to blow across Great Whale Island's green and purple moors, faintly at first, then stronger and stronger. The glassy blue water darkened as the sea breeze ruffled its surface into sparkling wavelets. Now *Loon* was tugging her weedy mooring line clear of the water. Over on Gull Island, flags began to lift in the strengthening breeze.

~~~

Wind! Enough wind to sail to Sei Island!

The twins thundered up the path through the dunes to leave float plans and make lunches. Sara ran toward *Rover*, the battered lapstrake dinghy that would take them out to *Loon* and *Phoenix*. *Rover* lay upside down just above the high tide line, her painter secured to a little mushroom anchor embedded in the sand.

Miguel was hurrying to help Sara turn the dinghy when his eye fell on one of the matted clumps of rockweed and eelgrass dotting the beach. The clump's rounded shape reminded him of his confiscated soccer ball.

With Miguel, to think was to act. His bare left foot lashed out. The matted tangle sailed a surprising distance down the beach and landed with a solid *thump*.

Neat!

Miguel looked around. He was surrounded by *dozens* of clumps of tangled weed. All he needed was a goal . . .

Twenty feet away, her back to him, Sara was bent over untying *Rover*'s painter from the little mushroom anchor. Her clean white shorts shone in the bright sunlight.

Unbelievable! She never turns her back.

Miguel gauged the distance to Sara's gleaming shorts, took three dancing steps, and launched a tremendous, left-footed kick.

~~~

Normally Argus-eyed whenever her little brother was nearby, Sara had forgotten completely about Miguel as she broke down the bowline in *Rover*'s painter. Sara was thinking that in a few minutes the twins would start hoisting *Loon*'s gaff, her white mainsail shaking beneath it.* A few boat lengths away, Miguel would pull the starter cord and *Phoenix*'s little outboard would roar to life. Then the two boats would drop their moorings, fall off the wind, and run through the Gut into Old Town Harbor. As always, *Phoenix* would let the slower *Loon* set the pace toward West Head's towering cliffs and the red-roofed Coast Guard buildings clustered at its base.

I bet Dad's out on the pier watching, Sara thought resentfully. *I bet he writes something down in his notebook.*

Perhaps some kindly fate would keep Dad safely stowed in his office as *Loon* and *Phoenix* sailed past the Coast Guard pier. Once clear of West Head, they would alter course for R "2." Up till today, the squat red bell buoy had been the outer limit of the two boats' voyages. Once they reached R "2," the four friends knew they had to turn back toward Old Town Harbor's sheltering arms.

But today, when the two boats reached R "2," the twins aboard *Loon* and Sara aboard *Phoenix* would note the time. Then *Loon* would alter course to starboard and point her bow at the distant blue dome of Sei Island. *Phoenix* would move abeam and, for the first time ever, the two boats would sail right out into Whale Sound.

The bowline fell apart. Sara straightened, the painter in her hand. A few minutes ago, she thought, Jon had been as excited as she was.

---

* Jon's schematic drawing on p. 104 shows *Loon*'s hull and rig.

"We're really going!" he had cried. "On our own!"

"On our own!" she had echoed.

Sara smiled as she thought of the glee in the brown eyes looking down into hers. . . .

Wait! Jon was looking down *at me?*

Sara suddenly realized that Jon had also grown huskier that summer. Jon had always been kind of skinny. Gangly, even. But Jon was gangly no longer. His shoulders were broader now after a summer of handling lobster traps aboard *Rosie*.

Sara began to wonder—did people change on the inside when they got bigger? *You must do* some *changing inside*, she thought. *But how much? Maybe you changed a lot when you grew up.*

Sara was just forming the hope that the Jon she knew wouldn't change too much when she heard a strange noise behind her—a noise like a strangled cry.

Sara whirled and crouched, one arm raised. Then she lowered her arm.

Miguel was standing on one leg like a chubby dark stork, both hands clutching his left foot to his abdomen. As Sara watched open-mouthed, he uttered another strangled cry and toppled sideways.

"*Miguel!*"

Sara's white deck shoes kicked up little sprays of sand. She dropped to her knees in front of the hunched figure. "What *happened*, Meeg?"

Miguel groaned.

"Did you step on a shell?"

Another agonized groan.

"Let me see," Sara commanded.

The bowed head shook.

"Come on, Meeg. I won't hurt you. Let me see. "

Sara prized Miguel's clutching fingers away from his foot.

"Oh, *Godfrey!*"

The toenail was split; the toe itself was already turning purple.

"*Double* Godfrey!" Sara repeated. "Oh, Meeg, that must *hurt*. How did you . . . ?"

Sara sat back on her heels and eyed the purpling toe. *No quahog shell did that.*

Sara thought of yesterday's loud crash at the house, the latest in a series of loud crashes that had punctuated a summer of expensive soccer practice. She thought of the confiscated soccer ball. She looked at the rounded clumps of rockweed dotting the beach.

"*I* know what you were doing. You were pretending you were playing on the All State team again, weren't you? You were using these seaweed things for soccer balls."

No response from the hunched form rocking on the sand.

"And," the relentless voice continued, "you were aiming at me. When my back was turned. Weren't you?"

That hollow groan *might* have been an agonized "Yes."

"All State team!" Sara snorted. "All State seaweed is more like it." Pleased with her wit, Sara thought of another good one. "All State garage windows." She laughed sarcastically. "*And* you go and kick the only thing on the beach with a rock under it. Serves you right."

Sara surveyed the clumps of weed near the stricken athlete. "That must have been some rock."

Miguel groaned.

Sara levered herself upright and toed some nearby clumps of rockweed. *Nothing here . . . nothing under this one . . .*

Then Sara's shoe hit something solid. She kicked the weed clump harder. Another shock as her toe hit something unyielding. The clump hadn't budged.

Sara studied the untidy clump. Whatever was hiding inside that weed didn't *feel* like a rock. A rock would move when you kicked it, unless it was a big boulder embedded in the sand. From living half her life on Shell-fish Bay, Sara knew very well there weren't any big boulders on its shores.

She knelt and pulled at the matted tangle. Something was pinning the seaweed to the sand. She began to pull the weed clump apart.

When she had discarded the last shreds of rockweed, Sara saw why Miguel's toe was so bruised. She reached down and tugged. She tugged harder, grunting with the effort. When the thing wouldn't budge, she dug around it, scooping the damp sand to the side. Several hard jerks with both hands wrenched it free. Then she turned to Miguel.

"It wasn't a rock."

~~~

The twins, laden with lunch boxes and a thermos, paused at the top of the dunes. Below them two dark heads were bent over something.

"What are they looking at?"

"Come on."

The twins ran down the path.

Sara was holding a golden crucifix whose arms ended in swirls of gold wire—swirls called filigree, Abbie remembered. A piece of purple glass was set in the center where the arms crossed the main shaft.

The cross must measure about twelve inches from top to bottom and at least six inches across the arms, Jon estimated. More, maybe, with those wire swirls. A gold-colored ring had been soldered to the top of the vertical arm.

"It weighs a ton," Sara said. She held it out to him. Jon put down his lunch box, took the cross, and nearly dropped it. "See?"

Jon hefted the cross. "Man! It's so heavy!" He looked at Sara. "Where'd you find it?"

"Buried under some seaweed," said Sara. "Right over there. Meeg . . ."

"Sara!"

". . . Meeg stubbed his toe on it. I really had to dig to get it up. There was only a little bit sticking up."

Buried under some seaweed. Only a little bit sticking up.

Jon's hands tightened around the dully gleaming cross. "Sara, do you know what this is?"

"No," she began. Then her blue eyes widened. "It's the de Parques'! The burglars buried it!"

Jon's eyes strayed to *Phoenix* and *Loon* tugging at their moorings. He looked down at the heavy golden cross. Then he looked at the others. "We've got to take it to Dad."

"Aw, *shoot!* We're *never* going to get to Sei Island! Just stick it up in your house and let's get going!"

Jon's voice was scornful. "Come on, Meeg. We're taking it to the police station. Dad and the guys have been looking for it since yesterday. Besides," Jon pointed, "you gotta get that toe looked at."

"Aw, *shoot!*" Miguel flung himself down on the end of an old drift-wood log. *Always bossing me around.*

"Jon's right, Miguel," said Sara. Abbie nodded.

All of them against me, Miguel thought tragically. *All of them. Like always. Nobody cares about my toe. Just sayin' that.*

"Okay if we take *Phoenix?*" Jon asked. Sara nodded. "Miguel will row us out, right, Meeg?"

"Well . . . ," Miguel, who loved to row, levered himself off the log and started limping toward *Rover.* "I dunno. . . ."

"Hey, Meeg!"

Miguel stopped and turned. "Let's see."

Miguel extended his foot. Jon bent and studied the purple toe. "Godfrey, look at that color." He straightened. "That hurt a lot?"

Miguel looked at Jon.

"I bet. Say, Meeg. Wash it off, okay? That's just a little cut, but there's sand in it."

No longer angry at Jon, Miguel waded into ankle deep water and balanced on his right foot. He winced as he swished his left foot back and forth. Then, as he swished, Miguel felt the sand shift beneath his right foot. He looked down through the foam-flecked water. His right foot was planted across a deep groove in the sand. When another little wave surged in, Miguel could feel the edges crumbling under his toes.

Behind him Miguel heard crunches and scrapes. The others were dragging *Rover* to the water's edge. He turned and limped through the shallow water toward the little dinghy.

Phoenix Meets Thresher

P*hoenix* bounced through the tidal swirls in the Gut and shot into the smoother water of Old Town Harbor.

"Ease her off, Meeg!"

Phoenix's twenty-horse outboard engine was mounted in a well just forward of the steering station. Miguel twisted the black throttle grip, and the little engine's high buzz dropped to a steady hum.

The green dory was moving sedately across a harbor rimmed with peaked and gabled roofs, weathered shingles, crowded docks and wharves, flagpoles, and signal masts. To starboard the high sun shone on the conical roofs of the beach club's cabañas. Colored pennants lifted lazily in the freshening breeze. Ahead lay a dense thicket of masts and nets: fishing boats sheltering at the town dock or unloading their catches at the fish market. To port lay the nearly landlocked Pond and its flotilla of pleasure boats, many of them off-island sport fishermen with tapering outriggers, down for the start of the famous Great Whale Island Striped Bass Derby. From one minute past midnight tomorrow morning and throughout the next two weeks, Great Whale's curving southern shore would be dotted with anglers launching their bass plugs into the surf while the sport fishermen hunted along the edges of Horse and Luce Shoals.

At the southern end of the Pond, the Old Town police boat was moving slowly through the fleet, its blue light flashing. And there was another strobe light: a chunky utility boat was coming alongside a cabin cruiser. A blue-uniformed Coast Guardsmen climbed aboard and followed the owner below.

"Still looking," Abbie said.

"Still looking," her twin echoed.

Then Jon spotted varnished masts towering over the other boats in the Pond. "Cap'n Ben's back!"

Before Abbie could answer, a shrill horn echoed off the high bluffs of West Head. The dory's crew turned. A long, low motor vessel was entering the harbor. Her black hull shone dully in the bright sunlight.

"*Thresher*," Jon said.

The others nodded.

As the *Thresher* rumbled slowly past the town dock, old Captain Look emerged from the harbormaster's shack and stared. He did not wave.

Captain Look and the four friends knew the black boat well. So did everyone in Old Town. *Thresher* had a buff-colored steel mast supporting a jib crane stepped against the after end of her dark red wheelhouse. On the after deck, lashed to a low cradle, lay a high-sided, beamy, flat-bottomed, all-purpose boat Great Whale Islanders call a "sea skiff." A powerful outboard engine was mounted on its transom, its massive shroud canted forward over the sea skiff's cockpit so that the propeller would clear the deck. A tiny outboard engine was fastened next to it on the transom. When the sea skiff was needed, *Thresher*'s crew would attach her three-part wire bridle to the jib crane, hoist her clear of her cradle, swing her outboard of *Thresher*'s hull, and lower her into the water.

Though they couldn't see *Thresher*'s stern from this angle, the four friends knew that her varnished transom bore a black silhouette of the

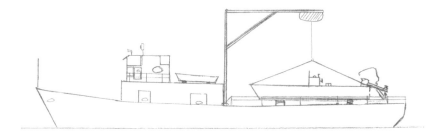

Miguel Selph's pencil sketch of *Thresher*, the day the four friends encountered her on their way to the police station. *Thresher*'s hull was, of course, black. The trolling engine appears clearly next to the huge main engine aboard the sea skiff.

long-tailed thresher shark, its body curved, its mouth stretched wide to consume the prey it had killed with its deadly, scythelike tail.

The larger vessel approaching *Phoenix*'s starboard side had the right of way. Sara called, "Neutral, Miguel . . . reverse . . . neutral."

As the dory slowed and stopped, white water seethed under the black vessel's stern and flooded toward her bow. *Thresher* began to pivot on her keel, swinging her stern so that she could back into her berth at the finger piers. As *Thresher* pivoted, her bow swung toward *Phoenix*. A door in the port side of the wheelhouse banged open, and a tall figure strode onto the wing of the bridge wearing a leather vest but no shirt. The man glanced briefly at *Phoenix*, then leaned outboard over the railing to look astern. His right bicep, Sara noticed, was disfigured by a dark stain. On his belt, in the small of his back, Sara saw a long knife in a leather sheath.

At a bellow from the bridge, two crewmen hurried through a door in the port side of the cabin house. A blubbery figure with bulbous arms waddled hastily toward the stern while a gigantic hulking man strode onto the anchor deck and bent over behind the bulwarks.

Before the *Thresher*'s stern pivoted away from the dory, Miguel jumped to his feet and pointed. "Did you see the sea skiff's new engine? It's *huge!*"

Miguel imagined himself aboard the sea skiff, one hand holding the wheel, the other closing over the smooth throttle knob. His hand moved. . . . The huge engine bellowed. . . . The long hull lifted, settled on a plane, and bounded from wave to wave. . . .

Miguel's shrill voice soared over the rumble of the diesels and the softer buzz of his idling outboard. "I bet she *flies!*"

A head and shoulders rose above the *Thresher*'s forward bulwarks. The hulking crewman grasped the port bulwark with both hands and leaned forward.

The sun riding high above Old Town Harbor fell squarely on the wolfish face staring down into *Phoenix*. The dory's crew saw a thin, pointed nose, a jutting jaw, cadaverous cheeks, a crooked, scarred lower lip, a scraggly black beard ruffled by the breeze, and a gold earring glinting through lank dark hair.

The hulking man ran his eyes over the twins sitting on the forward thwart, then over Sara standing at the steering station. The eyes then fastened on Miguel, still on his feet and still pointing after the sea skiff, now shielded from their view. The man bent forward, as if to get a better look at Miguel.

Miguel's hand started a friendly wave, then dropped to his side. He sank onto the midships thwart. *Why is he staring at me like that? His eyes . . . they're like black stones.*

The diesels rumbled and *Thresher*'s bow dipped. A voice bellowed. The wolfish face vanished.

"Okay, Miguel."

The boy did not move.

"Miguel!"

Miguel started. *Thresher* had docked. The way to the police station was clear. He turned quickly to the engine well. The outboard's idling hum deepened, and *Phoenix* moved slowly through the sparkling wavelets ruffled up by the freshening southwest breeze.

The Authorities
Take Charge

Sergeant Vernon Maciel clicked off the squawk box and smiled at his visitors. "Okay, kids. You heard the chief. Two minutes." Sergeant Maciel looked at the cross lying on his desk. "I bet he gives you four."

Vernon picked up the cross, placed it in a large accordion file, and strode down the brightly lit hall. The crew of the *Phoenix* hurried after him.

~~~

As he half-ran after Sergeant Maciel, Jon was thinking, a little nervously, that Chief Cooper on duty was very different from his father at home.

Off-duty and at home, Dad was the most affectionate of fathers, with a wonderful sense of humor. In uniform and on duty, Chief Cooper was a no-nonsense police officer who treated everyone impartially. Not insensitively; just impartially. And that included his twins.

Four summers ago, while attempting to bean his fleeing sister with a pear, Jon had broken a windowpane in the home of the venerable Miss Sophonisba Wimpenny, Old Town's town clerk and notary public. Then he had run away.

As luck would have it, Miss Wimpenny happened to be looking through that very window at Jon Cooper chasing his twin frantically into her backyard when a pane of glass shattered and a small, very hard green pear fell into the kitchen sink. Shaken but unhurt, Miss Wimpenny called the police station.

"It's an island," Chief Cooper told Jon when he had run him to earth. "We all know each other. If I start playin' favorites, my reputation is dead. So is law enforcement. Let's go see Miss Wimpenny."

Great Whale Island soon learned that Old Town's battered police cruiser had drawn up before Miss Wimpenny's cottage on Peirce Lane and the uniformed chief and his small son had vanished inside. The Island also learned that Jon Cooper had labored in Miss Wimpenny's garden until he had paid for a new windowpane—and his misdeeds.

"The bad thing was runnin' away," his father had told him. "It's the worst thing you can ever do. Never run away."

~~~

Chief Cooper smiled quizzically at his visitors. "Mornin', Jon, Abbie." He nodded to Sara and Miguel. "Didn't expect to see you two until after supper." Chief Cooper looked at his watch. "You say they found something, Vernon?"

Sergeant Maciel took the cross out of the accordion envelope and placed it in the center of the green blotter.

The chief perched his reading glasses on his nose. He bent forward and inspected the gold cross and its purple gem glowing in the cold office light. Then he reached forward, took the cross in both hands, hefted it, nodded to himself, and placed the cross back on the blotter. The chief leaned back in his chair and looked over his glasses at the four young people standing before his desk.

"Chief, I uh . . . I stubbed my toe on this cross. It was buried under some seaweed. On our beach." Miguel stuck out his bare foot.

Chief Cooper glanced down over his glasses. *God of war*, he thought. *Will you look at that toe.*

But he said only, "Mmmph," opened his desk drawer, pulled out a tan folder, extracted a sheet of paper, and scanned it. Halfway down the sheet he muttered something. Marking the place with his right forefinger, the chief glanced from the cross to the typed sheet, then back to the cross. Then he replaced the sheet, closed the folder, took off his glasses, and looked up.

"Well, Vernon." The chief smiled slightly.

Sergeant Maciel nodded. "Ay-up." "Ay-up" means "yes" on Great Whale Island.

The old swivel chair creaked as Chief Cooper stood. He looked briefly at the four friends. "Okay, kids, take *Phoenix* back through the Gut and meet us at the beach. I want to see exactly where you found it." The chief handed the heavy cross to Sergeant Maciel. "Stick it in the office safe, Vernon. I'll tell Josie to take the desk. Let's go."

Chief Cooper and Sergeant Maciel strode out the office door and turned down the hall.

"Dad! Dad!"

Chief Cooper did not turn or slacken his stride.

Jon tried to catch up. "It's the de Parques' cross, right, Dad?" he called to his father's back.

But Chief Cooper was speaking to a patrolman at the front desk.

"It's the de Parques'," Sergeant Maciel whispered. The four friends clustered around him.

"What else was stolen?" Sara wanted to know.

"Stuff like this cross. Some old coins. Everything was in two of those canvas bags the banks use to carry money. No one had any idea the de Parques were sittin' on stuff like this. Never said a word to us. Musta brought it with them when they came over in June. They were goin' to take it all to a museum in Boston next week." Sergeant Maciel winked at Miguel. "Your cross mighta come from a Spanish treasure ship."

"Treasure!" Miguel breathed. "For *real?*"

Sergeant Maciel nodded. "Solid gold," he whispered. He bent closer to his young friends and pointed to the purple gem. "It's an am-ee-thyst," he mouthed. "A huge am-ee-thyst."

The four friends goggled at the purple stone.

Abbie looked up at Sergeant Maciel. "Did you catch them?"

Sergeant Maciel looked cautiously toward the front desk. His back still turned, the chief was leafing through some papers.

"No," the sergeant whispered back. "No suspects. No clues, even. Mr. and Mrs. de Parque didn't hear a thing. No one in Old Town or over on the Bay saw or heard anything that night. No one except Mrs.

Atherton." Sergeant Maciel grinned. "You know Mrs. Atherton? Out near the Opening?"

The four friends nodded.

"*She* heard somethin'. She's always hearin' somethin'. A little outboard this time. Maybe fifteen minutes before midnight on Wednesday . . ."

Miguel looked up from his toe and frowned at the ceiling.

". . . and then another little outboard a while later. She said the outboards sounded 'suspicious.'" Sergeant Maciel grinned again. "Someone fishin', prob'ly."

The four friends nodded. Everyone would be fishing all day and all night now the Derby had started.

"All set, Vernon?"

Sergeant Maciel jumped. Chief Cooper was staring at the huddled group.

"We were just asking about the burglary, Dad," Jon said quickly. Sergeant Maciel was already spinning the dial of the big black safe. The four friends drifted toward the chief. "No clues, huh, Dad?"

Chief Cooper shook his head. Then he rubbed his eyes. "Not until now," he said. "The cross is our first piece of evidence."

"No suspects either?"

Chief Cooper frowned. "No, Sara," he said curtly.

An image of the wolfish face flooded Miguel's mind. Once again the dead black eyes stared down at him. "What about those guys on the *Thresher*?" he blurted.

The chief turned and looked down. "We already thought about them, Miguel," he said, sounding surprised. "Far's we can tell the *Thresher*'s crew is clean."

"How do you know, Dad?" Jon asked.

The chief's eyes narrowed.

"We're interested, Dad," Jon protested.

As he returned his father's gaze, Jon noticed—not for the first time that summer—that their eyes were almost level with each other.

"This goes no further, you understand?" The chief's voice was as stern as his eyes. "I shouldn't be telling you *anything*."

"We promise, Dad."

"Surf casters saw the *Thresher* go north through Butler's Hole at 5:45 p.m. on Wednesday—that was about six hours *before* the burglary."

"Oh."

"The *Thresher* docked at the Gardners Port Marine Terminal between 9 and 10 p.m. Wednesday evening. She was still there Thursday afternoon when a *Clarion* photographer was taking pictures at the terminal. I talked to him." The chief rubbed his eyes again. "The *Clarion*'s doing a feature on shipping activity in Gardner's Port."

"Oh," Jon repeated.

"That's not all. Witnesses saw *Thresher* go south through the Hole at about 8:20 Thursday evening—last night, in other words—almost twenty-four hours *after* the burglary. No way the surf casters could have missed her coming back, even in the thick weather. She was sounding her fog signal. Must have been heading for their cove over on Porpoise Island. They're off the list. Perfect alibi."

"They just passed us in the harbor," Jon volunteered. "They're docked at the finger piers."

The chief nodded absently, then pointed toward the door. "Okay, you four, off you go. Miguel, you want to come with us?"

Miguel shook his head.

The chief nodded. "Meet you at the beach, then. Mind the store, Josie."

"You Can't Go Near the Graveyard. . ."

Evening, Friday, September 1

The long light of evening was fading. The drought-brown lawn lay in full shadow, but just offshore, lit by the last of the westering sun, *Loon's* varnished spars and white sail stops glowed against the dark water of the bay. *Phoenix* swung in short arcs at the end of her mooring pennant.

A mob of herring gulls burst from the water and shrieked after a young bird with a crab dangling from its beak. Overwhelmed, the speckled gull dropped the crab, settled near *Loon*, and primly folded its wings. Sara watched the screaming gulls chase each other toward East Head, then turned away. The air was growing chilly.

The sharp odor of cooked onions hung in the kitchen's warm air. Sara's mother was standing at the kitchen counter preparing a tray. Her chunky little brother sat on a footstool by the wood stove brooding over the ice bag on his left foot. Her tall, blond father was just putting his uniform cap on the shelf in the hall closet and loosening his black tie.

Alan Selph smiled at his daughter. "Chief Cooper tells me you've had quite a day." He sank into the low easy chair opposite Miguel. "Tell me what happened this morning."

"Dad, we've already told the chief. And Mom."

Alan Selph eyed Sara. "Well, what about a short account? Oh, Marie, that smells good!"

"I kept it hot. Go ahead, Sara. Dad needs to hear it from you."

Sara sat at her end of the sofa and hugged one of the pillows. "Okay, okay." Once again she began the familiar tale. "Dad, the wind was just starting to fill in so we got ready to sail over to Sei. Miguel just happened to stub. . . ."

~~~

". . . And the chief said we shouldn't say anything to anyone about the cross."

Her narrative finished, Sara hunched over her pillow, stared across the kitchen, and waited for what she knew was coming.

Alan Selph wiped his mouth and folded the napkin. He sat forward in the easy chair, his blue eyes worried. "Godfrey, no. Don't say a word to anyone. Think of the consequences if the wrong people heard you'd found that cross." He leaned back and propped his sock feet on the coffee table. "I'll call Tom later. Just to be sure he doesn't think there's any danger."

Consequences! Always consequences! What are these "consequences" that only he can see? These dangers that never come?

While Marie Selph told Alan about Chief Cooper's unexpected arrival in the Selph's driveway that noon, Sara's eyes ran over the ranks of family photographs on the mantel. An ornate gilt frame in the center of the mantel contained a formal tintype of her great-grandparents Marie and Miguel Dias, dark-skinned Azoreans who had come to Great Whale Island in the nineteenth century. They had died before Sara was born.

Next to them stood Mom's father and mother, Eduardo Dias and his wife, Carolina, who was also descended from Azoreans. They lived on the mainland now but always came back to Old Town for Christmas.

Ranged among the Diases were framed photographs of the blond, blue-eyed Selphs. The largest photo on the mantel showed Alan Selph, a handsome Coast Guard lieutenant in dress whites smiling at his beautiful dark-eyed bride, née Marie Dias.

She's still beautiful, Sara thought.

Sara and Miguel had rose-brown skin, brown hair, and blue eyes. "You have the best of both of us," Marie Selph liked to say.

Sara's restless eyes moved from the mantel to the Packish Fuel Company calendar hanging beside the telephone. The page for August, its thirty-one days filled with scribbled reminders, scrawled times, and marginal entries with arrows pointing to their dates, each X-ed out as the month advanced, had vanished. In its place hung September's five rows of fresh white squares with no writing in any of them except one—in the square for next Wednesday, the sixth, Mom had written SCHOOL!

Sara thought of the two-room school housed in the old Great Whale Island Grange. Long-vanished island boys had carved their names deeply into the slanted oak tops of the iron-framed desks bolted to the wide-planked floor.

Sara sighed. What can you learn sitting in iron rows doing "exercises"? Listening to the pendulum wall clock ticking the day away . . . itching to burst free . . . to do what *you* want to do . . . read what *you* want to read.

Sara looked again at September's neat rows of clean white squares. She frowned.

Time doesn't look like that. The weeks aren't stacked on top of each other.

Sara imagined September's piled-up squares as a long row of white stepping-stones dwindling into the hazy future. She saw herself marching up the endless path of white stones, one stone for each day, each step leaving a black footprint on the white stone, the lengthening trail of black footprints stretching away behind her. . . .

Sara started. Her mother was smoothing the fine hair over her right ear. Alan Selph smiled across the coffee table. "Penny for your thoughts, Sara."

"Just thinking," Sara said. She gestured at the calendar. "Does time really look like that, Dad? Rows and columns?"

Her father's blue eyes followed hers. "Huh," he said. "What *does* time look like? Interesting question. Never thought about it."

Sara heard his puzzlement. She imagined trying to explain how she saw herself walking steadily up those white squares into the future. *He'd never understand.*

Instead, she said, "This weekend's our last chance to go to Sei Island. We were going today, but then the cross. . . ."

Sara looked across the coffee table. "All summer we've been sailing around and around the harbor and the Pond. Turning back at number 2. We're almost out of time!"

Alan Selph's blue eyes regarded his daughter. "Sara. All that time you were sailing around and around the harbor, you were gaining experience and skill. You know that. You're good boat handlers now. Last week you handled the fog exactly right. You've earned your permission."

Alan Selph was smiling as he solemnly raised one finger. "Tomorrow's the day," he intoned. "You're going to explore new waters. On your own. And nothing's going to stop you. I feel it in my bones."

Then Alan Selph's smile faded. His voice was grave. "Just remember, Sara."

Sara stiffened.

"You can go anywhere in Whale Sound from Luce Shoal to Point Despair—but you can't go near the. . . ."

"Dad!" Sara was startled by the vehemence in her own voice. "We *know*," she said more moderately. "We know. You told us last night, too. We're not supposed to go near the Graveyard."

Alan Selph's blue eyes held his daughter's. "Just want to be sure you understand, Sara." He picked up his day-old copy of the *Clarion* and snapped it open. "That channel is a death trap," said the voice from behind the paper. "Off limits."

Sara stared angrily at the big black letters on the *Clarion*'s front page. *How does he know it's a death trap? What makes it a death trap?*

Then an idea banished Sara's questions, and her anger with them. She plumped the pillow against the sofa's arm and rose. "Okay if the twins come over, Mom?"

Marie Selph looked at the kitchen clock. Her dark eyes smiled at Sara. "Why not? The evening's young. What are you three going to do?"

"Four," came a voice from the footstool.

Sara sighed. She picked up the wall phone's earpiece. "Talk about the trip, Mom . . . 158, please, Miss Paul."

Great Whale Island had no dial telephones in 1950. When you wanted to call someone, you picked up the earpiece of the old-fashioned, two-part telephones the islanders were still using. That connected you to the duty operator working in Old Town's telephone office, who would say, "Number, please." When you told the operator the number you wanted, he or she would connect you using a manual plugboard.

Sara heard the tinny croak of the Coopers' phone, then a *click*.

"Hi, Abbie. You and Jon want to come over?

Chart 471

"He said it *again*!" Sara cried. "Just now. 'Don't go near the Grave-yard,'" she mimicked. "It's all he can say! Like a parrot! 'Don't go near the Graveyard! Dangers! Consequences!' Night after night!"

Sara's blue eyes sought Jon's. "What *is* it about the Graveyard, Jon?" She gestured at the large chart spread out on her carpet. "It's just this blank blue place."

Jon pointed to six asterisks in the patch of blue. "Rocks. Dad said the Graveyard's a death trap."

"That's exactly what *our* dad called it!" Sara cried. "A death trap."

"Then that's why we can't go there," Abbie said reasonably. "Besides, who needs it? We can go anywhere else we want. All the way from Luce Shoal—" Abbie pointed to the western end of Whale Sound— "to Sei Island and Point Despair. Anywhere we want but the Graveyard."

Sara was still studying the asterisks in the patch of blue. "Six rocks and it's a death trap?" Her blue eyes narrowed. She bent closer to the chart. "Jonno—Right under where it says *The Graveyard.* See the real little numbers?"

"Yeah?"

"You ever seen chart 471?"

"Nope."

Sara looked at her brother sitting on the opposite side of the large chart. "Meeg, is chart 471 in that pile?"

Miguel turned and pawed through the heap of rolled-up charts he had brought down from the rack in his turret room. When he turned back, he was holding a tightly wound tube dappled with mildew. Miguel pulled at the free edge, but the chart sprang back upon itself.

"Grab it, you guys."

With Sara and Jon holding the free edge, Miguel unrolled chart 471. The four friends weighted the corners with a sneaker, a worn-out monkey's fist from the station now ending its days as a doorstop, a chipped piggy bank full of pennies, and an old sash weight from the floor of Sara's closet. Then they knelt at the bottom of the chart.

"Man!" Jon said.

Abbie's ponytail bobbed. "It *is* a death trap!"

Chart 471 was choked with a thousand asterisks and stars—cartographers' symbols for "Rks, Bldrs, and Foul ground." But the four friends saw something else—or three of them did.

Over the previous winter, Commander Selph had taught the twins and Sara how to read charts. Among other valuable lessons, they had learned that the color blue on coastal charts designates shallow water and that white designates deeper water. He had cautioned them, moreover, always to check the depths on any chart they were using. On small-scale coastal charts (covering large areas), thirty feet may be the cutoff between the white and the blue, between deep and shallow water. But on large-scale charts like 471, which show a small area in great detail, the cutoff can between the white and the blue can be as shallow as ten feet.

"You've always got to know the chart you're using," Alan Selph had reminded his young pupils. "These depths are crucial to your safety."

The four friends saw immediately that most of the Graveyard depicted on 471 was predominately blue. But the Graveyard was not *all* blue. A thin white dogleg of deeper water ran through its rocks and boulders.

Sara looked up at Jon. "It's like a little lane through the rocks!"

Jon ran his finger south down the lane of white. "All the way from Butler's Bay down to Whale Sound. How deep is it?"

Sara bent over the chart. "Thirty feet down at the Whale Sound end," she intoned. "Twenty-eight, twenty-six, twenty, eighteen . . . Jon! Here's a six-foot place with a blue circle around it. Right after the eighteen."

"Must be a rock."

"I guess. Fifteen, fifteen, fifteen . . . "

Miguel took up the litany. "Still fifteen feet at this bend in the Lane." Miguel's high voice rose. "Then it gets shallower: ten, ten— here's another six with a blue circle, then a ten again, then twelve, twenty, twenty-six, thirty-two, twenty-eight, forty, and you're out into Butler's Bay."

Detail from Chart 471
(modified)

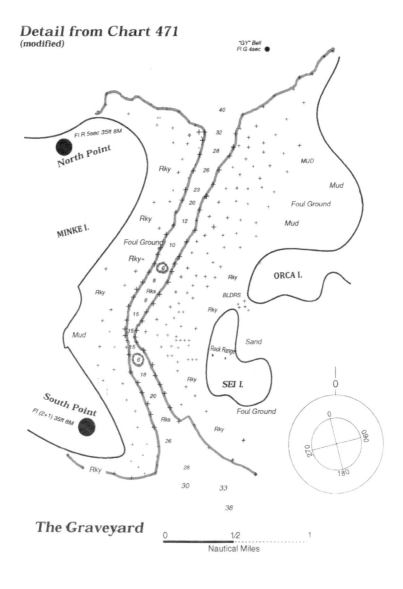

The Graveyard

0   1⁄2   1

Nautical Miles

~~~

"The shallowest place is six feet," Sara said. She sat back on her heels and looked at Jon.

Jon looked into Sara's shining eyes. *She's really excited about this Lane,* he thought.

Sara turned back to the chart and ran her finger up the lower part of the white lane through the rocks and on to the northern tip of Minke Island. Without turning she called, "Jonno! The Lower Lane is lined up right on North Point Light. I wonder . . ."

Sara ran her finger down the upper leg of the Lane. "Yep! The Upper Lane is lined up with South Point Light."

Sara sat back on her heels and studied the thin white ribbon through the asterisks and stars. "Plenty of water," she mused. "For small boats, anyway. And you've got those lighthouses lined up with each leg of the Lane. They're your bearings—to keep you inside the Lane. The only tricky part would be turning her at this Bend." Sara tapped the thin white Lane at the place where it changed direction. Then she sat back on her heels. "I wonder why they won't let us go in there."

Abbie looked up from the chart. "Current, I bet."

"More than in the Gut?"

"Maybe not *more,* but the Gut doesn't have all those rocks. Maybe the current shoves you into those rocks. . . ."

"But if you were real careful and stayed lined up on those light-houses . . ."

Sara's voice faded. She bent motionless over the chart, almost as if she was memorizing the contours of the thin white Lane threading the Graveyard's dangers.

"Well, anyway," Abbie said. "Doesn't make any difference how many lighthouses there are. We're not supposed to go in there. . . ."

Abbie's voice trailed away. She looked at Sara's alarm clock, then at Jon. He nodded, then looked at the slim figure bent over the chart.

"What time tomorrow, Sara?"

Sara's was moving her index finger slowly down the Lane from But-ler's Bay toward South Light.

"Sara?"

"What? Oh!"

Sara scrambled to her feet and started to say something about tomorrow morning. Then she snapped her fingers.

"Say . . . What about all of us going in *Phoenix*? It's going to be southwest tomorrow—maybe fresh southwest."

Jon had been looking forward to making this first passage to Sei Island in his beloved *Loon*. He had never told Sara, but sailing was much more fun than droning along in a powerboat.

Then Jon thought about *Loon* punching her way through the chop on the long beat home. *Phoenix* would have to punch into those seas, too, but *Phoenix* could head directly into the wind. *Loon* had to beat to windward. It would be a very long sail back. He looked at Abbie. She nodded.

Jon fished in his jeans pocket and extracted a few crumpled ones, his pay for a disappointing week of lobstering. Sara's white shorts yielded a dollar bill. Abbie was holding a five-dollar bill, her stunning bonus from a very grateful mother of three young children.

Miguel looked out the window. He had already squandered his weekly dime on Tootsie Rolls. And he had not shared any of them with the others.

"Enough for gas," Jon said. "Ten tomorrow?"

"Nine-thirty," Abbie advised. "The gas dock gets busy on the weekends. And this is Labor Day weekend."

At the door Jon turned. "See you tomorrow, Sara."

Sara didn't answer. She was staring down at chart 471.

"'Night, Sara."

Sara did not look up. "'Night," she said absently.

The door clicked shut.

The Lane through the Graveyard

Midmorning, Saturday, September 2

The cresting sea lifted *Phoenix*'s stern, heeled her to starboard, and sent her surfing down its foaming slope. The dory's hull thrummed as she rushed ahead, the wave from her nearly buried bows hissing away on either side. As the wave passed under her, *Phoenix* lifted her bows, heeled back to port, and settled into the trough.

As the next sea loomed, *Phoenix*'s stern rose and she heeled to starboard. Then she was surfing down the large sea, a great bow wave fanning out to either side. A small rainbow glittered in the spray suspended over the stern wake.

Another sea picked them up and shot them ahead. As they roared down the forward slope, Jon looked astern at the pale gray bulge of East Head. Sighting across the box compass, he took quick bearings on the orange and white fairway buoy swaying in the waves a half mile astern, then on the brilliant white cone of South Point Light broad on the port bow. Using his index fingers and the compass rose printed on a chart laminated to a piece of plywood, Jon traced his rough lines of position. Where his fingers met was—*approximately*, he reminded himself—*Phoenix*'s position. He checked his battered watch: 10:46.

"About a mile to go," he called over his shoulder. Then he faced forward again.

Sei Island's bald dome was shining in the bright sun. To reach the cove they would swing wide around Sei's southeast corner, then putter straight in to the beach. Would it be crowded with boats this Saturday of Labor Day weekend? Or would they have the hard-packed white sand to themselves?

While Jon studied Sei Island, Abbie was peering through the binoculars at the entrance to the Graveyard. Propelled by the brisk southwesterly breeze, white-crested waves were driving northward into the Lane and up to the Bend, but the flood tide running down the Lane pushed them back to the south. Caught between wind and current, the waves leaped upward in irregular peaks and crests. Abbie could make out violent eddies where the tide-driven water was checked by something beneath the surface. She remembered Chart 471's crosses and asterisks and the two blue circles with "6" inside them.

Abbie refocused the glasses. Two long lines of foam marked the edge of the channel. Between them lay the narrow Lane, where the current boiled and eddied. Outside the lines of foam, the water was quieter, its surface a myriad of ripples winking cheerfully in the clear light. But Abbie knew what lurked beneath the lightly rippled water beyond the lines of foam.

"I can really see where the rocks are! It's like there's fences at the edges of the channel. You can't miss 'em."

"What's the time?" Sara called.

"Eleven." Jon checked the note he had scribbled on a corner of the chart. He looked up at Sara. "High water's quarter to one."

Phoenix's course was carrying her northeastward across the mouth of the Graveyard. The four friends stared silently at the passage opening up to port.

"Guys!" Sara's voice was excited. "The Lane's lined up with North Point light! Just the way the chart says!"

Sara looked down at the others. Her voice casual, she said, "Just for fun . . ." Then Sara pulled her port tiller line.

As *Phoenix* turned to port, she rolled to starboard. The fresh sou'wester now blowing across the dory's beam began to cool the crew's sun-warmed cheeks. Then the bow of the green dory was lined up on the tip of North Point light, just visible above the trees on the island's crest. *Phoenix* was headed directly between the two lines of foaming water that marked the edges of the narrow Lane.

Sara glanced down at the compass. "Course up the Lane is north. More or less." She looked up from the compass. The lines of foam converged steadily until, some distance ahead, they appeared to meet.

That must be the Bend.

Glancing from compass to lighthouse, from lighthouse to compass, Sara kept the little dory's bow pointed at the exact center of the channel.

Abbie lowered her binoculars and looked to starboard. Sei Island's bald dome was moving steadily down the starboard side. Abbie looked to port. The stubby white lighthouse on South Point moved steadily down the port side.

If we keep going, she thought, *we'll be inside the Graveyard. But we'll be turning soon.*

But *Phoenix*'s bow remained fixed on North Point light.

Abbie turned and looked at Jon. Then they both looked back at the helmsman.

"Sara?"

Sara's mouth was set. Her shining blue eyes never left the white lighthouse.

"Time to turn, Sara!"

Sara shook her head.

Abbie and Jon cried out together, a confused babel that sounded like, "Dad said we can't no way Graveyard's a death trap we *can't!*" The last two words were a desperate shriek from Abbie.

Sara's blue eyes blazed at the twins. "I'm skipper. We're going in there. Jon," she ordered, "you and Ab help me read the water. Meeg, stick to that engine and listen up."

"Sara!" Abbie wailed. "We're not sup*posed* to!"

"We're *going* to!" Sara yelled back.

Jon didn't speak, but his brown eyes were troubled. He braced himself. *Phoenix* began to bounce as she entered the turbulent waters of the Lane's lower leg.

~~~

Her round face worried, Abbie scanned the disturbed, eddying waters of the Lane and the quieter water on either side of the narrow Lane. To port she saw the densely forested hump of Minke Island rising steeply from a rocky shore. To starboard two weather-beaten pines, their branches pointing northeast, clung to the rocky dome of Sei Island.

As the current swashed and roared along the edges of the narrow channel, its turbulence punctuated by deep sucking sounds, Sara could feel the rudder vibrating through the tiller lines. Whenever a tidal eddy threw *Phoenix* toward one line of rocks, Sara would saw violently on the tiller lines to bring the dory back to safety. One eddy threw *Phoenix* perilously close to a huge rock whose roiling wake, Sara noticed, made it seem to be forging upstream through the turbulent water.

After yet another struggle to fight *Phoenix* back into the middle of the Lane, Sara was exhausted. Desperate to flee, she looked at the foaming edges of the rocky channel, now so frighteningly close to port and starboard.

We've got to keep going, she thought despairingly. *There's no room to turn.*

"Sara!"

Jon was pointing ahead.

Phoenix was nearing three steep rollers that spanned the narrow channel. The rollers didn't move like most waves. They seemed to be fixed in place. Just in front of the odd standing rollers Sara could see a deep swirling depression filled with foam-flecked eddies. She remembered the blue circle around the numeral "6" . . .

Sara's knuckles were white as she gripped the tiller lines. *What should I do? More power? The engine's going almost flat out!*

"Miguel! Goose it!"

The twenty-horse engine roared as Miguel twisted the throttle. The little dory leaped forward and dropped sickeningly into the swirling hollow. The bow then jumped skyward as the reverse eddy threw the dory up onto the first roller. The twins, sitting forward, clutched at the gunwales. Sara, who was standing, fell forward, hitting both knees on the after edge of the engine well. Miguel was thrown backward off his thwart into the bilge but was up again in a flash. Then the current rolled the dory steeply and hurled her sideways toward the rocks to starboard. Water flooded over the starboard gunwale. Sara sawed desperately on her port tiller line. *Phoenix* would not answer her helm. As Sara opened her mouth to scream, the current threw the dory bodily to port and dropped her into the hollow on the far side of the first roller. *Phoenix*'s stern rose, and her bow buried itself in the swirling hollow. Solid water flooded over the bow. Abbie scrambled aft, the water halfway up her shins.

Phoenix's bow lifted sluggishly as she breasted the second roller. The engine coughed, coughed again, then resumed its steady hum as the bow dropped into the trough on the roller's far side.

Phoenix shipped only a little water as she wallowed over the third roller, the smallest of the three, then dropped on its far side into smoother water.

The lethal rollers behind her, *Phoenix* steadied on an even keel, rolling sluggishly as water sloshed about under the thwarts. Jon seized the galvanized bilge pump floating among the floorboards.

"Godfrey," Sara breathed.

"You okay?"

"Bashed my knees." Sara smiled wanly. "I thought we were going all the way over."

Jon looked at her for a moment, pumping steadily. Then he turned and faced forward.

The water-logged dory was nearing the turning point they called the Bend. The sucking, roaring edges of the channel were very close now. *Phoenix* lurched to port. Sara sawed on the starboard tiller line; the bow crept slowly back to starboard. A stream of solid water poured over the side as Jon's arms churned the pump handle. Miguel was hunched over his engine, his left hand clutching the outboard well, his right clamped around the twist throttle.

While *Phoenix* wallowed heavily through the turbulent current, Abbie was scanning the Graveyard's waters to port and starboard of the Lane. On one of her sweeps to starboard, she paused, fixed her salt-smeared binoculars on something, then turned back to Sara and pointed.

"Sara! Look at those rocks!" She pointed toward Sei Island, now abaft the starboard beam. "The ones with the red stripes."

The pump began to suck. Two more strokes and Jon laid it on the floorboards.

"One's up on the side of the hill. The other's down on the beach."

Sara stared to starboard. The red stripes on the two rocks were almost in line. She looked to either side, then ahead. The lines of foam were starting to bend to the northeast, just the way they did on the chart. Without realizing it, she had begun to steer *Phoenix* to starboard, following the contours of the narrow strait. Sara's clenched hands relaxed. Freed of water, a lighter *Phoenix* was easier to steer.

"Those striped rocks are a range," she told the others. "When they line up, you're at the Bend."

Moving slowly against the waning flood tide, *Phoenix* continued her gentle, curving turn to the northeast. Sara eased her starboard tiller line and took up the slack in the port. The Bend was astern. *Phoenix* was in the upper leg of the Lane now, still in the dead center of the channel. The water ahead of her was smooth, though eddied here and there where the current swelled over submerged boulders. To either side, the familiar lines of turbulent water roared over rocks at the edge of the Lane. Inshore, on either side of the Lane, the water was quiet.

"None of those awful rollers." Then Sara's voice rose. "Hey, lookit!"

Directly over *Phoenix*'s bow a bell buoy showed clearly against the blue sky.

Jon looked back at Sara. "It's a system. If you're coming in from Butler's Bay, you pass close to that buoy, aim at South Light, and that'll take you right down the Lane to the Bend."

"And when you get to the Bend, those two striped rocks tell you where to turn."

"Maybe those stripes show up in a searchlight beam. Like the reflectors on buoys."

Jon looked back at Sei Island. "I wonder who put the stripes on those rocks."

"Fishermen?"

"What fishermen would go through *this* place? They'd use Butler's."

Jon turned. "It's 11:45. How much gas we got left?"

Sara ducked down and peered under the after thwart. "This one's got a quarter left. The spare is full."

"Whoa! We've got a head wind and head sea going back. Ten minutes tops. Then we smoke for home."

Phoenix shouldered her way up the Lane toward the bell buoy out in Butler's Bay, the hull shuddering in the eddies that swirled over the submerged rocks. The current still surged and frothed along the edges of the channel, but the angry roar was fading. The Upper Lane was widening perceptibly. *Phoenix* had room to turn.

"Ten minutes!" Jon called.

"Neutral, Miguel!"

Sara pulled hard on her starboard tiller line. As the little dory lost way and turned to starboard, the waning current pushed her to the south. When the bow pointed at South Light, Sara called, "Forward. Half ahead," and the little twenty-horse resumed its steady hum.

Phoenix was running faster now, the last of the flood tide urging her back down the Lane. With most of the water pumped out, the green dory reached the Bend in much less time than it had taken her to battle up-tide to the turning point.

As *Phoenix* neared the Bend, Abbie monitored the two striped rocks. Then she looked back at Sara. "Coming in line."

Sara pulled on her port tiller line and *Phoenix* swung to port, away from the boiling water where the last of the flood tide fought its way around the rocky fangs at the edges of the Bend. Easing her port tiller line and taking strain on the starboard, Sara aimed *Phoenix* directly between the two lines of foam that marked the edges of the Lower Lane.

Abbie had been gazing back at the Bend ever since they turned. "Hey! There's something in the Bend." She leveled the glasses. "It's a pot buoy."

Jon turned to his twin. "You *sure?*"

Abbie refocused the glasses. "Red . . . yellow band around the middle . . . yellow pickup stick." She handed the binoculars to John. "It's a pot buoy."

Jon took a long look, then frowned. "Don't know those colors." He lowered the glasses. "Weird place to set a pot. Must've been towed under until the current went slack." Jon handed the binoculars back to his twin. "Good thing that line didn't snag the prop," he said thoughtfully.

Phoenix was coasting down the last of the flood tide toward the open waters of Whale Sound. The three standing rollers had shrunk to little bobbles. *Phoenix* bounced once, twice, a third time, and was through.

Now the channel was opening out. The disturbed waters at the edges of the Lane were further from *Phoenix's* sides. The rush and swirl had quieted.

Abbie reached down to unfasten the water-tight compartment under her thwart. "Let's get the oilskins on before we need 'em."

Phoenix was beginning to roll in the beam seas as she left the shelter of South Point. The four shipmates, now in yellow oilskins, black sea boots, and bulky life preservers, braced themselves against the roll.

When they were clear of the Graveyard, Sara pulled her starboard tiller line. *Phoenix* rolled heavily to port as she turned toward East Head and began to pitch into the short, steep seas.

Sara ducked a sheet of spray. Then she called, "Ab! How about steering?"

Sara slumped onto the floorboards, her back against the dory's side, her head resting against a cushion. She closed her eyes.

We made it through the Graveyard, she thought drowsily. *One little rough place . . . No death trap. No consequences.*

Then Sara heard her own voice saying, "I thought we were going all the way over."

The Meaning of Miguel's Dream

3:30 p.m., Saturday, September 2

Miguel's turret room was silent. The four friends were remembering how they answered the flurry of questions about their first trip to Sei Island.

It was great . . . swell. . . . Navigation was perfect. . . . Yeah, we started home a little early. . . . No, we didn't feel like going ashore . . . just putted around and explored and stuff . . . ate on the boat coming home. . . . Yeah, really wet . . . The pump worked fine . . . engine worked fine.

Sara's voice broke the troubled silence. "Did they believe us?"

Jon looked at Abbie sitting cross-legged next to him on the sisal carpet. Her round face was sad. Then the twins turned to Sara huddled in the old wicker chair that had once sat on Grammy Dias's porch.

"Yes," Jon said wearily. "They believed us."

"Why wouldn't they?" Abbie asked Sara.

Abbie dropped her eyes. Jon looked out the window.

A herring gull laughed raucously. Oystercatchers screamed as they skimmed Shellfish Bay. A distant engine coughed to life, choked, and died. *Loon's* halyards rapped a sharp tattoo against her mast. The minute hand of Miguel's new clock ticked up the dial.

Cornered by their silence, Sara turned on the twins. "What's wrong with you two?" she burst out, her blue eyes blazing. "There was just that one bad place. We *made* it, didn't we?"

The sandy blond heads did not turn.

"Well, *didn't* we?"

Jon looked up. "We almost *didn't* make it. We almost capsized. You said so yourself." Sara's blue eyes fled from his. "And we lied about it."

Sara's head whipped back. "We didn't say a *thing* that wasn't true!" she blazed.

"We told them half the truth and let them believe it was the whole truth," Jon shot back.

Sara glared angrily at Jon. Then she turned away and stared at the wall.

For a while the room was silent. Then Abbie looked up. "Sara?"

Sara's blue eyes narrowed. "*What?*" Her angry voice threw a towering wall around her.

"How come you wanted to go into the Graveyard?"

Abbie's voice was merely curious, Sara realized, not judgmental, and she knew it could have been. The anger in her blue eyes faded. She sagged in the creaking wicker chair, laid her head back, and stared at the ceiling. The others waited.

When she finally spoke, Sara's voice was no longer defensive. "It never occurred to me until I saw that channel through the rocks. On the chart." Sara raised her head and looked at the twins. "Then, when I saw there was a way through there, I just had to find out what the Lane was like. I don't know why. I really don't."

"Well, now you *know* what it's like," Abbie said feelingly. "And so do *we!*"

"We were pretty lucky," Sara admitted. She looked at Jon, her blue eyes sad. "I know we lied, Jon."

"Well," said Abbie seriously, "we won't ever lie again. Because we're not going into the Graveyard again."

"Never again," Sara echoed, her voice as serious as Abbie's had been. "We *know* what it's like."

Jon laughed.

"What's so funny?" Abbie cried. "We *do* know what it's like."

"I know," Jon said. "But I was just thinking. They can *tell* you the Graveyard's a death trap, but you don't really know it is until you see it for yourself."

"Well, we saw it for ourselves," Abbie said grimly. "*Phoenix* is too small for the Graveyard. Maybe a big boat could get through there, but poor little *Phoenix* just doesn't have enough power."

Sara was opening her mouth to defend *Phoenix* and *Phoenix*'s little engine—defend them playfully, not angrily, because her heart felt so much lighter—when Miguel shot bolt upright on his bed.

~~~

Oblivious to the drama unfolding next to him, Miguel had been sleepily reliving the glorious swoop and rush of the toboggan ride down Whale Sound toward Sei Island. He remembered the sickening plunge and the awful lurch when *Phoenix* was thrown to starboard by the standing rollers. He remembered his stomach churning in black despair when his beloved engine coughed once, then coughed a second time. He remembered the flood of relief when his engine resumed its steady buzz.

Abbie's faraway voice barely penetrated the vivid images flooding Miguel's mind, but penetrate it did. As in a dream Miguel heard, *Poor little* Phoenix *just doesn't have enough power.*

In seconds a train of complex associations flashed through Miguel's sleepy mind.

Phoenix *not have enough power?* Miguel waggled the much smaller, not quite so purple toe he'd hurt yesterday morning. *Shoot, they'd done fine today—after those scary rollers, anyway. They'd had enough power. Specially after the current slacked. At maximum current maybe they wouldn't have had enough, but big boats would do fine in there. Boats like Ferdie's* Rosie, *like the* Thresher's *sea skiff with that humongous engine . . .*

Miguel visualized the enormous swollen bulb of the two-hundred-horse engine, the trolling engine tiny beside it. *That* was power! Far more power than *Phoenix*'s puny little twenty-horse.

Another thought flashed through Miguel's sleepy mind: *Phoenix*'s twenty-horse must be about the same size as the sea skiff's trolling engine. Miguel knew that the sea skiff used the little engine for fishing at slow speeds. He imagined the sea skiff trolling for blues off Horse Shoal. The huge bellowing engine would be silent, and the little engine would be buzzing along just like *Phoenix*'s as it pushed that great big boat. Just buzzing along, Miguel thought sleepily.

The little trolling engine . . . buzzing along . . . buzzing . . .

Once again it was Wednesday night. Miguel remembered sitting bolt upright in bed listening intently for the buzzing noise that had woken him. The old clock's hands were pointing to midnight.

Midnight . . . buzzing noise . . . the little trolling engine . . . pushing the sea skiff . . . Mrs. Atherton out by the opening . . .

~~~

Miguel shot bolt upright. "They *did* it!" he shrieked. "I was right all along! They *did* it!"

The others spun toward him.

"And I know *how* they did it! I know *how!*"

"Who?" Abbie shrieked back. She looked wildly around the room. "Who did what?"

"What are you talking about?" Jon cried.

"The guys on the *Thresher!*" Miguel cried. "I know how they did it!"

"Did what?"

"The burglary!"

Abbie clutched her head.

Sara snorted.

Jon shook his head. "Miguel, you just . . . you just don't listen. It *couldn't* have been the *Thresher*'s crew. They were in Gardners Port. The chief talked to witnesses. A guy from the *Clarion* took pictures. C'mon, Miguel."

"Miguel." Sara might have been talking to a young, not very bright child. "Think about it. If the *Thresher* was in Gardners Port last Thursday night, how did it get back here to do the burglary. *Fly?*"

"Well, not *exactly* fly. Anyways, it wasn't the *Thresher* that came back."

The others stared at Miguel.

"He's gone soft," Sara said finally.

Miguel stood his ground. "You remember yesterday? How I pointed at the sea skiff and yelled how she must really fly?"

The others waited, their faces skeptical.

"I bet the *Thresher* went through Butler's Hole, put the sea skiff in the water when it was dark, stuck some of the crew into the sea skiff, and sent 'em back through the Opening to Shellfish Bay. With that flat bottom they could land right on our beach. Yeah, and when I was swishing my toe I felt this real faint skeg mark in the sand. With my foot. I saw it too. I didn't know what it was then, but I do now. Except it's gone by now," Miguel said sadly.

"Miguel," Jon said, "no one heard that huge engine. There's no way you can make that two-hundred-horse sound like the little outboard Mrs. Atherton heard."

"She heard the trolling engine. When they got near the Opening, they turned off the big engine and puttered the rest of the way on the little one."

Jon stared at Miguel, his eyes narrowing. "And puttered out the same way," he said slowly. "Just like a little boat looking for blues."

"It . . . it makes sense," Sara admitted. "It would've taken them about fifteen minutes to putter across Shellfish Bay."

Sara looked at her stocky younger brother. "How did you ever figure that out, Meeg?"

"I heard them."

"You *what*?"

"You know when you're asleep and you hear a noise, but you don't wake up? And your mind puts the noise in a dream?"

The others nodded.

"Last Wednesday I had a dream about this buzzing noise. The buzzing kept getting nearer and nearer, but when I woke up, nothing was buzzing. My clock said it was midnight. I thought I'd just dreamed about the noise, so I went back to sleep." Miguel's eyes were round. "The buzzing was the sea skiff's little engine. They must have shut it off just when I woke up."

"You woke up at *mid*night?"

Miguel nodded at Jon. "Just before." He pointed at the new clock. "When I went back to bed, the hands were pointing straight up."

"Wednesday?"

"Wednesday."

Jon looked at Abbie. "Wasn't it midnight Wednesday when Mrs. Atherton heard the little outboard?"

"Sergeant Maciel said a little before midnight. And another outboard later on."

"It was the same outboard," Miguel said. "The trolling engine on the sea skiff."

Abbie was clambering to her feet. "We've got to tell Dad."

"Yeah!" Sara began to struggle out of the wicker chair.

Abbie giggled. "I can't wait to see his face. Meeg finds the cross. We bring him the cross. Now Meeg's going to tell him who stole it. Come on, Meeg!"

The bearer of important news eased off his bed, wincing slightly as his left foot hit the floor. Sara and Abbie ran to the door. But Jon remained seated on the carpet.

Miguel looked down at the older boy. "You coming, Jonno?"

Jon looked across the room. The girls were already out in the hall. "Sara, Abbie," he called. "Wait up."

Jon turned to Miguel. "I think we better talk this over, Meeg."

"Talk what over?"

"What you're going to tell Dad."

"I'm going to tell him what I told you!"

"You're going to tell him you had a dream about a buzzing noise?"

"Well, yeah!" Miguel said defiantly. "I *am*!"

"And you're going to tell him you saw a mark in the sand?" Miguel nodded. "A mark that's not there anymore?" Miguel's brown face tightened. "And you had this vision about the sea skiff and its trolling engine?"

Miguel sank back onto his bed.

"Remember the Fourth of July?"

Abbie hugged herself to keep from laughing. When *Loon* and *Phoenix* were sailing by the bathing beach on the Fourth of July, Miguel had spotted something ominous close to the shore. His wild cries of "Shark! Shark!" had driven scores of beachgoers screaming from the water. When the police boat arrived, rifles at the ready,

Miguel's "shark" turned out to be the corner of someone's waterlogged swimming mattress.

Sara looked at her brother's angry face. "Miguel's right about the sea skiff," she told the others. "But we can't prove he's right."

"No," Jon said. "We can't prove it."

Miguel sank onto the edge of his bed. He stared out the window at *Phoenix* and *Loon*. He heard the scrape of chair legs, then creaks from the old wicker chair. Out of the corner of his eye Miguel saw Jon drop to his knees with something in his hands. He turned. The older boy was unrolling the big chart.

"What're you doing, Jon?"

Yesterday morning, Chief Cooper had not stopped when Jon had called after him, had not even answered. He had kept on striding down the police station corridor.

The Thresher's *clean, huh?* Jon anchored the top corners of the chart with his sneakers. *Perfect alibi, huh?*

Jon looked at the younger boy perched on the end of his bed. "We're going to figure out what they did with the rest of the stuff. Then we'll have something we can take to Dad. Something he'll *have* to listen to. C'mon, Meeg—gimme a hand."

~~~

Once again the four friends knelt around the big chart.

"You know Dad," Jon told the others. "The first thing he'll ask is how the sea skiff got back to Shellfish Bay without being seen."

The four friends studied the chart of Whale Sound. They knew there were only three ways to pass through the long chain of islands: narrow gutters too shallow for anything but kayaks, the well-traveled Butler's Hole, and the Graveyard.

Jon tapped the familiar patch of blue. "*Had* to be the Graveyard."

The others nodded.

"They wouldn't dare go through Butler's Hole. It's jammed with surfcasters. But no one would see them in the Graveyard. And it's the shortest route to the Opening."

"We got through there," Sara agreed. "If we did, they could've."

"But," Abbie reminded her, "we can't *say* that. . . ."

"We need proof," Jon said. "We really need proof that's the way they went."

"Hey!" Miguel cried. "The rocks!"

"What rocks?"

"The ones on Sei. With the red paint. *Someone* painted those rocks."

Light dawned in Jon's eyes. "The *Thresher*'s crew!" Then he frowned. "But we can't *prove* they did it. Besides, we're not supposed to know those stripes are there."

"Oh." Miguel looked glumly at his purple toe. "Yeah."

"And we can't prove it was the sea skiff that landed on our beach."

Abbie's voice was reluctant, as if she were speaking against her better judgment. "Well, what about—" And there she stopped.

The others waited.

"What about the newspaper?"

"*News*paper?" Jon asked. "*What* newspaper?"

"Remember what Dad said? About the *Clarion*'s story on shipping? The photographer?"

The others nodded.

"Well," Abbie said slowly, almost unwillingly. "If there's a photograph with the story, and *Thresher*'s in the photo but the sea skiff's not aboard her . . ."

Jon scrambled to his feet. The others heard him clattering down the circular iron staircase that led to Miguel's room. A moment later the Selphs' screen door banged.

~~~

Chief Cooper was snoring quietly on the sofa, the wreckage of that day's *Clarion* draped across his stomach and lying on the floor. Jon's eye fell on a section tented against the sofa. Careful not to step on the paper, Jon bent to take a closer look.

Betty Cooper looked up as Jon tiptoed across the den. "Mom," he whispered. "Okay if I take the sports section over to the Selphs'? Want to check on the Red Sox. I'll bring it back."

Chief Cooper sighed deeply. Betty Cooper smiled and nodded.

With exquisite delicacy, Jon lifted the sports section from his father's gently heaving stomach. Then he bent and silently lifted the section that had first caught his eye. Holding both sections so the pages would not rustle, Jon tiptoed from the room.

Back in Miguel's turret room, Jon tossed the sports section into a corner, then knelt and spread out the section he had lifted from the floor beside his sleeping father. The others knelt beside him.

The headline read, "Banner Year for Gardners Port Marine Terminal." Ed Mello, director of the Marine Terminal, was quoted at length. A box beneath his picture (Ed talking into the phone and writing something on a pad) summarized how much cargo had been landed each month and where it had come from. Another photo showed Ed out on the Terminal pier pointing at a large cargo vessel that filled the center and left side of the picture.

But the four friends' eyes were fixed on a second vessel in the right background of the photograph. A much smaller vessel—and a very familiar one.

The *Thresher*'s deck and upper works showed clearly above the edge of the pier. There was the wheelhouse and, abaft the wheelhouse, the cabins; there was the mast and the jib crane; and there, barely discernible, was the sea skiff's cradle. But the cradle was empty.

"You were right, Miguel." Abbie stared solemnly at the picture. "You were right."

"Boy-oh-boy-oh-boy." Miguel's eyes were round.

Then Miguel remembered the wolfish face staring down at him over the *Thresher*'s bulwarks and the dead eyes boring into his.

~~~

"Okay," Jon said. "Miguel was right. What do we do now?"

Sara's eyes were shining. "Figure out where they took the rest of the stuff!"

"Sara!" Abbie cried. "We've got to tell Dad! It's the cops' job to figure out where it is."

Jon looked at his twin. "Tell him what? The picture doesn't *prove* those guys did the burglary. It's a clue, but it's not proof. But if we can figure out where they took the stuff, and it's there, that's an even bigger clue."

"We can't —" Abbie began, but Jon cut her off.

"We can," he said. "We can figure out where they hid the stuff. Then we'll decide what to do about it."

Still seeing the dead black eyes, Miguel cried, "It's at their camp on Porpoise! Where we can't go!"

"Can't *be*!" Sara cried. "They'd never have it near them. That's the first place the Chief would look. If he ever started to suspect them."

"*I* know!" Abbie said hopefully. "I bet they took it to the mainland today. I bet it's gone for good!"

"Would they do that right now?" Jon questioned. "Right now they've got the perfect alibi. Nothing connects them to the burglary. Dad said so. Besides. If they went back to the mainland right after Dad was asking all these questions about them, someone would call him for sure."

"Yeah, but sooner or later they're going to have to go for the stuff," Sara said.

Jon stared at the chart. "We know Porpoise is out. They'd never hide it there. Or on Great Whale either. Too many people. Someone would see them for sure when they came back for it."

"Pilot's got all those cottages filled with summer people. "

"Beluga's some kind of religious campground. People wandering around in bedsheets . . ."

"Minke's owned by those rich people from Boston," Sara put in. "They've got their own guards. They let surfcasters on the island, but they have to stay on the shoreline down by the Hole."

"Orca's got that secret navy base. Out near Point Despair. Whole island's patrolled." Jon sat back and finished the inventory of the Little Whale Islands: "Sei's all rock except for the cove, and there are boats in and out of there all summer, like us today."

Jon looked around at the others. "*Every* place is out," he said gloomily.

"But it's got to be *somewhere*," Sara cried. "It can't be *nowhere*!"

Abbie twisted her ponytail. Sara tapped her knee with a yellow pencil. Jon stared down at the chart as if willing it to speak. Miguel hummed softly to himself as he ran his eyes over the mustard-colored land shapes and the irregular bands of blue water girdling the islands.

"Maybe we should do this another way."

The twins looked at Sara.

"We've been staring at the chart trying to figure out which of the Little Whale Islands it's on. Maybe we should try to figure out what kind of place you'd hide something you stole."

"Somewhere no one would see them," said Jon.

Sara nodded. "A place no one ever goes."

"And some place no one *would* go," Jon added, "so you could be sure no one would see you when you came back to get the stuff."

"Because it's too far. . . ."

"Or it's hard to get to. . . ."

"Say, what does 'quarantine' mean?"

The others stared at Miguel. "What are you talking about *quarantine* for?" Jon cried indignantly. "We're trying to figure out where the stolen stuff is!"

Miguel pointed to a little mustard-yellow blob in the northwest corner of the chart, far from the other islands. "'Quarantine Island,'" he read. "What's it mean?"

Jon peered at the chart. "Oh. *That* quarantine. Quarantine means you can't go there because of diseases." He and Sara turned back to the Little Whale Islands.

"Quarantine Island used to be a leper colony," Abbie told Miguel.

"What's a leper?"

"Someone with a disease. An *awful* disease. Your nose and your fingers and your toes fall off." Abbie's voice rose over Miguel's shrill disbelief. "They do *so* fall off! So do your ears. *Everything* falls off. They put you with all the other lepers someplace far away so no one will catch it from you. That's what Quarantine Island was for. Miss Dillon said the buildings are still there but they're abandoned. No more lepers. But no one wants to go there. 'Fraid they'll catch it."

Jon sat up and looked at his twin.

Abbie's round face grew solemn. "Miss Dillon read to us from this book of stories people used to tell about the island. Ghost stories and stories about how you'll die if you go there. Miss Dillon called it 'a lot of superstitious nonsense.' "

Abbie shivered deliciously. Then she started to tell Miguel one of the Quarantine Island ghost stories Miss Dillon had read to the ninth grade last Halloween.

"Sara!" Jon whispered. Sara's blue eyes looked into his. He pointed to the solitary little mustard-colored blob. "An abandoned leper colony people are afraid to visit . . ."

Sara ran her pencil eraser around the Quarantine Island's coastline. "No harbor for cruising boats . . . and it's off the route to Gardners Port."

". . . and it's far enough away from Porpoise so you wouldn't think of the *Thresher*'s crew goin' there."

"You wouldn't think of it, period," Sara whispered. "We didn't until Meeg asked what 'quarantine' meant. How far is it?"

Jon hunted for his dividers and stepped off the distance from the Opening to the Graveyard, then from the Graveyard to Quarantine Island.

"Twenty-point-two miles. Call it twenty. Only an hour at full speed with that big engine. More like two hours if they stayed on the little outboard until they were well away from the Opening. They'd get there way before sunrise and hide the stuff. Yeah, and later on they'd meet the *Thresher* on her way back from Gardners Port."

"So the sea skiff would be back aboard *Thresher before* she went south through the Hole on Friday," Sara whispered excitedly. "She'd look just the way she looked Thursday afternoon when they went north through the Hole!"

Jon returned the dividers to their case. He and Sara turned toward the others.

Miguel was staring at Abbie, his mouth half open, his eyes round. Abbie's voice thrilled with menace as her story reached its climax. "Slowly it approached the window of the sleeping child," she intoned. "It pressed its noseless face and fingerless hands against the. . . ."

"Hey, Ab," Jon interrupted, "listen up."

~~~

Miguel finally gave in. "Yeah," he said unwillingly, "I guess you're right. Where else could it be?"

Abbie was appalled. "There's no *way* we can find out," she cried. "*Is* there? It's much, *much* too far for us. We're not even allowed to go through Butler's Hole! Besides," she added, piling up obstacles, "tomorrow's Labor Day. School starts Wednesday. We've got lots to do before then. . . ."

Sara and Jon looked at her silently.

"You've got to be kidding." The old wicker chair creaked as Abbie shrank back against its cushions. "In *what?*"

Jon looked out Miguel's southern window at a towering varnished mast glinting through the trees. He looked at his watch. Then he turned to the others.

"It's 4:30. I'll check in with Mom. Then I'm going over to see Cap'n Ben." Jon looked at Sara. "Anyone else want to come?"

Cap'n Ben Hears a Story

4:45 p.m., Saturday, September 2

Captain Benjamin Pease, descended from Great Whale Island's first settlers, had retired from fishing and bought the large cruising yawl *Manitou*. He was in the charter business now. Every summer he and his clients cruised the North American coast from Great Whale Island east to the maritime provinces of Canada. Around Labor Day he returned to Great Whale so that he and his crew could refit *Manitou* and then get some rest. In late October, toward the end of the hurricane season, *Manitou* and her crew went south and resumed chartering in the Caribbean. In April or May they returned to Great Whale for another rest and refit before the summer's cruising began.

On this Saturday before Labor Day, Cap'n Ben Pease was sitting in the cozy wood and brick kitchen of his saltbox house in the cul-de-sac at the end of Try Works Lane. Copper-bottomed pots and pans hanging from a wrought-iron frame glistened in the late afternoon sun. The kitchen smelled of coffee, cocoa, and spices, overlaid by the faintest whiff of tar.

Though he was alone in the world, his wife gone early and his two grown sons "moved off," Cap'n Ben had company this afternoon. Sitting with him around the blue and white checked tablecloth were three young people he had known since they were toddlers. The boy and one of the girls had just finished making a complex and, to Ben Pease's practical mind, strange request.

"It would mean a lot, Cap'n Ben." Jon Cooper's voice sounded manly and competent. "It's our last chance. School starts Wednesday."

"We'll bring the picnic," Sara said eagerly. "Lots and *lots* of food!"

Ben Pease was not given to flights of fancy. Commercial fishermen and charter captains do not build castles in the air. But while he was a practical man, Ben Pease was not unkind. He did not say, "I'm sure Chief Cooper will be able to get along fine without our help," or "Now you kids run along home and leave these things to the experts."

He studied the three young faces. He hadn't seen them since the previous summer. The three older kids, with Sara's chubby little brother tagging along, were always out in that green dory and the white sloop, sailing up and down the harbor or around Shellfish Bay.

They were all taller. Taller and older-looking. Sara's rose-brown features were becoming distinct—high cheekbones, a straight nose, thin lips, her wide-set blue eyes looking at him intently from under dark bangs. The twins had blunter features: snub noses, round cheeks, freckles, sandy blond hair. Jon's hands, folded quietly on the checked cloth, were large, the fingers muscular. Smaller than her twin brother, Abbie radiated the same dependable sturdiness, the same compact, quiet strength, though this afternoon her open, round face was worried.

Cap'n Ben's washed blue eyes were set in a ruddy, weathered face creased with wrinkles. The wrinkles deepened as he fished his shore pipe out of the pocket of his clean khaki shirt and reached for a match.

"Interesting," he mused. Clouds of sweet tobacco smoke swirled toward the polished copper lamp hanging from the ceiling. "Anybody else know about this idea of yours?"

"Just Miguel," said Sara. "Mom made him stay home so she could ice his toe."

"But you *did* tell your folks about coming to see me?"

"Oh yes, sir," Jon said. "They said we had some nerve but okay if you had the time and we'd bring the picnic."

Cap'n Ben puffed silently. Before the Great War, when he was about twelve, he'd started helping the family make money peddling to Old Town's housewives the fish he'd caught and the clams he'd dug. There'd been no room in that life to be a kid: to invent stories, believe them, act them out. . . . But he did remember, faintly, what it felt like when summer ended and the schoolhouse loomed.

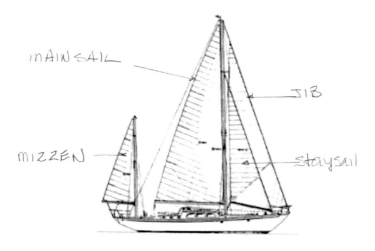

Sail plan of a 1950s-era yawl with a double-headsail rig

"What if the stuff is there but it's guarded?" he asked. "Thought about that?"

"If there's anyone there, we leave. Fast. We come back here and tell Dad." Abbie sounded scared.

Cap'n Ben nodded. He puffed awhile in silence, remembering two young boys climbing *Gertrude's* mast. A thin cry drifted down to the cluttered deck where he and his mate were hoisting out the glistening black bodies of swordfish. "Hey, Dad! C'mon up! You can see all the way to the lightship!"

He had not gone up. No time . . . had to get those fish ashore, take on some ice, gas, grub . . . head back out . . .

Cap'n Ben looked at the picture on the wall opposite. Himself as a young man. His young wife. The two little boys in their arms. He thought of the empty rooms above and the quiet in the house. He wasn't due to move *Manitou* over to the shipyard until Thursday. He puffed on his pipe. Maybe Horace and Albert would come along.

Cap'n Ben looked at Jon Cooper. He looked at Abbie sitting across the table from him, her round face serious. Then he turned and winked at Sara. He was smiling broadly around his pipe stem.

Sara's eyebrows lifted. Her blue eyes widened, and she opened her mouth.

"Who knows what we'll find out there on Quarantine? Hey, now, Sara, you stop that!"

But Sara wouldn't stop hugging him, and now Jon was stammering his thanks and trying to shake his hand. Even Abbie was smiling a little.

"Ham and cheese sandwiches," Cap'n Ben said. "Sweet gherkins." Cap'n Ben thought for a minute. "Potato salad would be nice, too."

The Passage to Quarantine Island

Late Morning, Sunday, September 3

Cap'n Ben glanced aloft at the windsock, then down at the compass in the polished brass binnacle. He looked quickly to port—the black can was just abeam—then astern—nun "2" was well back on the starboard quarter. He straightened. Horace was standing by the main sheet, Albert by the staysail sheet, and Miguel and Abbie by the jib sheet. He knew Sara and Jon were stationed behind him, ready to trim the mizzen.

Cap'n Ben's gnarled hands turned the mahogany wheel a few spokes. The big yawl heeled to starboard as she began her turn to port. The fresh sou'wester came further and further forward until it was blowing directly on her beam. Though Cap'n Ben had not said a word, winches turned and sheaves rumbled in wooden cheek blocks as the crew trimmed the sails.

When *Manitou*'s bow neared a humped blue silhouette on the horizon, Cap'n Ben eased his wheel to starboard— "meeting her," it's called—and *Manitou*'s turn to port slowed until her bow was leveled at Quarantine Island.

When she steadied on course, the powerful yawl was on a close reach, battling her way across big seas that lifted and rolled her to starboard. When her spoon bow crashed into a large sea, the hull shuddered and spray sheeted across the foredeck. The genoa jib and the staysail were wet across the foot and well up the luff.

Bracing himself against the roll, Cap'n Ben shifted his gaze from windsock to compass, from compass to the horizon ahead, and from the horizon to the water on either side. *Manitou* rolled deeply to starboard. Another sheet of spray flew across the foredeck.

Cap'n Ben looked over his shoulder. "Jon," he called. "Stop staring at Sara and take the wheel. Yes, you, Jon. Close your mouth and come heeah. You want to ship aboard, don't you? Never mind how I know. Take the wheel. That's it. Steady on that island up ahead theyah. Boys, let's get the jib and main off her."

Cap'n Ben meant "Come here" and "ahead there," of course, but like many tidewater New Englanders, he tended to drop the letter "r" from words like "here" and "there." So did most other Great Whalers, including the twins' father.

~~~

Jon eased the wheel a spoke or two and watched *Manitou*'s bow move slowly back to the point he had chosen on the low silhouette of Quarantine Island, still a good six miles ahead. Under staysail and mizzen alone, *Manitou* was sailing more easily—no longer smashing her way into the seas but rising and falling with them.

Jon watched carefully as another big sea loomed off the port bow. In *Loon* he would be bracing himself for the jar when the little sloop's bow was thrown skyward, preparing to duck the shot of spray he knew would be coming at his head. He held *Manitou*'s wheel steady. The big yawl forged majestically ahead, her hull rising smoothly as she surged up and over the wave. Jon didn't move the wheel more than a spoke to keep her on course. Not a drop of water had come aboard.

"You're gettin' the feel of her," a voice said in his ear. "Some different from your little sloop, I bet."

Jon grinned and nodded.

"Keep her as she's goin'. You stay on the wheel while we anchor. Just do what I say."

Jon nodded again. "I will, Cap'n Ben."

Me on the wheel while we anchor? Jon thought, trying to project an air of nonchalant seamanship. *Godfrey!*

~~~

Manitou was sailing toward a cove on Quarantine's southeastern shore where she would be sheltered from the smoky sou'wester.

As *Manitou* approached the thirty-foot curve, Horace and Albert dropped the staysail. When the sail was on deck, Cap'n Ben told Jon to put his wheel over hard to starboard and hold it there. Under mizzen alone, *Manitou* circled once, then again, losing way with each turn. As she circled, Horace and Albert were hoisting out the big fisherman's anchor on its davit.

Half way through the third turn, Cap'n Ben told Jon quietly, "Now put her right into the wind and hold her theyah."

The big yawl was barely moving as Jon steered her dead up wind. As *Manitou* eased slowly forward, Cap'n Ben was watching the water over the starboard side. When the bubbles were barely moving past the hull, he looked forward and nodded. Horace nodded back, and the anchor plunged into the clear blue water of Butler's Sound. As *Manitou* began to gather sternway, the little mizzensail, acting like a weather vane, kept her bow pointed into the wind.

Cap'n Ben nodded again, and Horace threw the brake lever on the yawl's capstan. The anchor chain stopped clanking overboard. *Manitou*'s bow dipped as she set her hook in the soft mud. They were there.

Cap'n Ben stood for a moment, looking at the island's skyline to port and starboard.. When he knew *Manitou*'s anchor was holding, he turned to his young crew.

"Time to go ashore!"

Quarantine Island

Jon and Abbie were holding the short straws and the right to explore the island.

To Miguel and Sara fell the bitter duty of serving as a screen for the explorers. To convince any watchers that the *Manitou*'s arrival at Quarantine was a harmless late-summer picnic, Miguel was to collect beach glass ("Aw, *shoot!*"). Sara was to spread the checked cloth on a flat rock down by the shore and place the picnic basket prominently upon it. Then she was to sunbathe on a striped beach towel.

"Sunbathe? *Me?*"

"Just keep your eyes open," Jon reminded her, "but don't let on that's what you're doing."

~~~

Jon and Abbie strolled through the heather and bracken with Cap'n Ben dramatically, as sightseers do, to different features of Quarantine Island's topography: the scattered rocks deposited by the glacier, a large depression that protected some scrub oaks from the wind, and the purple heather that grew everywhere on the eastern side of the island.

Although the sightseers appeared to be wandering aimlessly, they were actually working their way toward some tumble-down buildings huddled on the northeastern slope of a knoll in the middle of the island.

As they strolled, Cap'n Ben fished around for topics to keep his young friends chatting naturally.

"Geography! Youngsters today don't seem to know anything about geography."

Then his voice dropped. "When we get near those buildings, you, Abbie, ask me to go in. I'll say no. Pester me." *Might's well go along with the game. Starting to believe it myself.*

"Oh, we study geography," Jon retorted loudly. "This year it's Asia. Last year it was South America. Do you know where Patagonia is, Cap'n Ben?"

"Been there," Cap'n Ben retorted. "South coast of Argentina. Blue whales. Sea lions. Orcas. Abbie. Did you say you're studyin' French?"

Abbie nodded.

"Say somethin'," Cap'n Ben demanded.

Abbie looked fixedly at a distant cloud, her lips moving. Then she produced a shrill statement which she said was French for a pen belonging to someone's aunt which had gotten, for some reason, into a garden.

"Good thing to know how to say," Cap'n Ben said encouragingly, trying not to smile. "Might come in handy. Never know."

The three explorers were now only thirty feet from the largest of three dilapidated buildings. Its door lay across a crumbling brick walk flanked by thickets of brambles. The few remaining shutters hung crookedly. Any paint on the weathered shingles had long since vanished. The little burying ground south of the buildings, most of its fence rotted away, was overgrown with bracken and heather. A few bleached wooden grave markers stood crookedly. Fallen grave markers lay here and there among the tangled ground cover.

Cap'n Ben poked Abbie.

"Oh! Cap'n Ben," Abbie implored, "let's go in! I *love* to explore old buildings. Please *please* let's!"

"Don't know 'bout that," Cap'n Ben replied righteously. "Not our house. Y' don't go into other people's houses, even deserted ones."

"Aw, come *on*, Cap'n Ben," Jon whined loudly. Abbie choked with laughter, then doubled over when Jon dug his elbow into her side. "No one lives here!" Jon cried. "These houses were abandoned years ago."

Cap'n Ben appeared to relent. "Well, maybe. But only for a minute. Long sail home. Tide turns soon."

"I wonder if this is where the lepers lived," Abbie cried.

~~~

Miguel couldn't find any beach glass. Not a shard. So he was trying to see how many different kinds of shells he could find. There were millions of them lying all over the beach, but it was getting more and more difficult to find new specimens. He walked slowly along, back bent, searching for something new among the purple and white fragments of quahog shells.

Miguel finally straightened and turned toward the water.

When Miguel had last looked—before he had lost himself in shells—he had seen only *Manitou* lying to her anchor and distant white triangles of sails retreating toward the mainland.

Quarantine Island

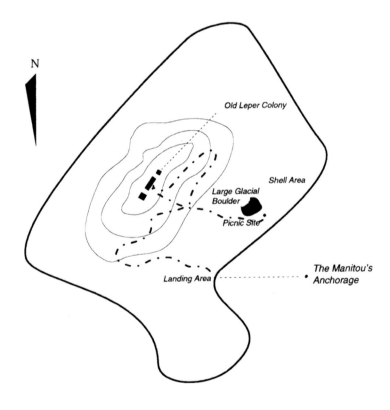

N

Old Leper Colony

Shell Area

Large Glacial Boulder

Picnic Site

Landing Area

The Manitou's Anchorage

· — · — · — · — · — · — · — · — Route of exploration party

Now a white powerboat was lying dead in the water a mile offshore.

Continuing his turn to his left, as if he hadn't seen anything, Miguel bent down and placed *Manitou*'s bucket on the pebbly beach. When he straightened, he turned his head further toward the northwest, away from the white boat. Then he skewed his eyes as far to his right as he could manage. A sudden flash! Another flash! The sun's rays were bouncing off something aboard the white boat.

Still facing northwest, Miguel dropped his hand from his eyes and bent to retrieve his shell bucket. Then he began to stroll back toward Sara's flat rock. Every few yards Miguel set down his bucket, stooped, and picked over the stones and broken shells at his feet. Each time he did this, he skewed his eyes to his left.

The fourth time he bent over, the white powerboat was gone.

Miguel's mouth was cottony dry.

~~~

The three explorers stopped in the doorway and peered into a large room with crumbling, rough-plastered walls. Decades of summer heat had baked and warped the floor's bare boards, creating uneven gaps from which nail heads protruded. A rusted metal cot with sagging springs stood under a western window whose wavy panes were streaked with dirt and cobwebs.

The warped floorboards creaked as Cap'n Ben stepped into the dreary room. Abbie and Jon tiptoed after him. On the wall to their left, the twins could make out faint scratches in the crumbling plaster. Despair hung in the musty air.

"The island is really nice," Abbie whispered. "But this is awful." She thought of the lepers pictured in Miss Dillon's book. "I wonder if lepers wrote those things on the wall."

"Kind of bare," Cap'n Ben commented dryly. He looked sideways at the twins and laid a finger against his lips. "Wait here," he said. "I'll take a little walk around."

Cap'n Ben started slowly into the room, putting his weight down carefully. He kept next to the walls. Once he stopped to study the crumbling plaster. "One of the Mayhews wrote this. Before the Civil War, musta been." He looked back at the twins. "Interestin' piece of Great Whale history out heeah."

Cap'n Ben skirted the walls until he reached the western window. He peered through the dirty panes, glanced down at the rusty cot, turned to resume his circuit of the walls—then stopped short and turned. He stooped to look down, not at the cot itself, but at the floor beneath it. The twins heard a muffled exclamation, something like, "Well, for . . ." Then Cap'n Ben was kneeling, his face close to the uneven boards.

After a minute, Cap'n Ben straightened. He seemed to think for a minute. Then he spoke.

"Come on over, you two. Walk where I walked."

The twins skirted the crumbling walls until they stood near the rusty bed frame.

"Look," Cap'n Ben said softly. He pointed at the floor.

Abbie nodded. "Scratches. Someone's dragged the cot."

"Ay-yup." Cap'n Ben grunted as he stood. He moved carefully to the head of the cot. "If I tell you to run," he said quietly, "you make straight for that door and run fast or the beach. Understand?"

Abbie's eyes widened.

"Grab a-holt of the other end, you two. When I give the word, pick up your end and let's walk this bed out from the wall . . . one, two, three, lift!"

The twins grunted. The rusty metal frame was surprisingly heavy. They shuffled sideways with their burden. "Now down . . . good."

Then Cap'n Ben was squatting again and feeling along the floorboards. His weathered hands suddenly stopped moving. "For the luva Pete," the twins heard him mutter. Then Cap'n Ben looked over his shoulder.

"What *is* it?" Jon hissed.

Abbie felt her throat tightening.

Cap'n Ben pointed to a long, straight seam in the flooring. "Looks like a trapdoor." He shook his head. "Would you believe it? A trapdoor . . ."

Cap'n Ben fished a rigger's knife out of the pocket of his khaki trousers, the kind with a large, blunt-headed blade and a marlinspike.

He inserted the blunt head of the blade under the edge of the trapdoor and bore down.

A section of flooring rose an inch. Cap'n Ben bore down again and was able to slip his fingers under the door's edge and lift it a few more inches. Then he shifted his grip, raised the door with both hands, and laid it back against the wall. He peered down into the black hole. Abbie moved closer to her twin.

"Ladder," Cap'n Ben said quietly. "Looks new."

Cap'n Ben folded the blade of his knife and stowed it in his pocket. He drew out a small flashlight. The twins saw the beam flash across cellar's earth floor. "Looks pretty empty." Cap'n Ben shone the flashlight beam into the dark northern corner. "Just busted up furniture. Old plaster. Might's well get goin' . . . *Hold* on!"

"What is it?" Abbie gasped.

Cap'n Ben leaned across the trapdoor opening and braced himself with his left arm against the south wall of the old house. With his right hand he moved the flashlight back and forth. Then he levered himself away from the wall and stood. "Something's flashin' in the light."

Cap'n Ben looked at the twins. Though his face was set, he winked one blue eye. "Might's well find out for sure. I'm going down to have a look. Here, Jon. Shine the light back behind the ladder. Now move the light." Cap'n Ben guided Jon's hand back and forth. "There! See it?"

Jon nodded.

"Hold the flashlight on it nice and steady. I'm gonna need both hands. Abbie, grab Jon's belt so he doesn't fall down that hole." Jon flinched as Abbie's knuckles dug into his back. "Never hear the end of it if you broke your neck . . ."

The ladder creaked, and Cap'n Ben's head sank into the gloom. The thin beam probed back and forth. *Glint—glint.* Jon locked his disc of light onto the glinting thing, whatever it was.

"I'm down."

The twins heard Cap'n Ben's sea boots crunching the broken plaster. When he reached the far side of the ladder, the flashlight shone on his back. When Cap'n Ben moved out of the flashlight's beam, the thing glistened again.

Cap'n Ben edged along crab-wise, trying to keep out of the flashlight beam. He stooped, stretched out his arm, straightened up, and turned so that the flashlight beam shone into his cupped hands. He stood there a moment, peering down. Then he was standing directly below them looking up.

"Turn off the light, Jon. I'm comin' up."

Cap'n Ben's head and shoulders rose above the edge of the trapdoor. He rested his arms on the floor and looked up at the twins. A shred of gray cobweb dangled from the brim of his cap. His lined face was so grim that he looked like a stranger.

"What is it?" the twins whispered.

Cap'n Ben opened his right fist. In his palm lay a gold coin. He handed it to Jon, then clambered onto the worn floorboards.

The edges of the coin in Jon's palm were irregular, as if the coin had been worn by use. One side was embossed with a robed man standing in an old-fashioned ship. The man was wearing a crown and carrying a shield.

"There's writing on it," Jon said.

Cap'n Ben picked the coin out of Jon's palm with one hand and with the other perched his dangling glasses on the end of his nose. He turned the coin as he studied the letters.

"Looks somethin' like 'EDWARD DEI GRA REX ANG.' Then there's a bunch of letters that don't make sense. But EDWARD means Edward. DEI means God. GRA I don't know, but REX means king and I'm bettin' ANG has something to do with Angles and Saxons. I'm bettin' this coin was made for Edward King of England."

Cap'n Ben thought for a moment. "No number, either. That guy who quit bein' king back before the war was Edward Number Eight. This coin musta been made for the Edward Number One." Cap'n Ben looked over his glasses at the twins. "Now that must go back a spell. "

"So we were right," Jon said, looking back at Cap'n Ben. "This must be from the de Parques' coin collection."

"Oh, *no*," Abbie whispered.

"Oh, *yes*," Cap'n Ben answered, his voice grim. "Isn't this what you expected?"

Abbie shook her head. "It was just a kinda game."

Cap'n Ben looked even grimmer. "Not a game anymore." He thought for a moment. "If it ever was. Now, is that it? Or did they leave some more of the stuff here?"

The twins looked at each other.

"Only one way to find out." He handed the gold coin to Abbie. "Don't lose that, now."

Abbie quickly handed the coin to Jon, who put it in the pocket of his khaki shorts. The ladder creaked as Cap'n Ben's head sank into the gloom. Abbie opened her mouth to scream at him that they should go back to Old Town . . . *quickly* back to Old Town!

"Where's that light?"

Jon crawled back to the edge of the trapdoor, Abbie still clinging to his belt, and aimed the light down into the hole.

"Shine it back where I found the coin," the gruff voice ordered.

Cap'n Ben sidled around the ladder again, but this time he got down on his knees and ran his hands across the earthen floor.

"Nothing heeah," he muttered. Captain Ben turned his head. "Jon! Shine the light farther back and to the right. See where I'm pointing?"

"Hold on, Cap'n Ben."

Jon scuttled sideways to the south end of the opening in the floor. Abbie scuttled along behind him, holding on to his belt like grim death. Jon leaned his left shoulder against the bottom end of the trapdoor where it rested against the south wall. Abbie braced herself behind him and took a fresh grip on his belt.

"You can let go now, Ab. I'm okay."

"No!" Jon's light wavered as Abbie's knuckles ground deeper into his back.

"What's going on up there?"

Jon took a deep breath and steadied the light.

"That's *it*! Keep it right there." Cap'n Ben crawled forward, feeling the cellar floor with his hands. Jon heard a sharp *snick!* And then, in the beam of his light, Jon could see flashes of movement as Cap'n Ben begin to scrape at the earth in the far corner of the cellar. As the knife in his left hand gouged the cellar floor, his right swept the loose earth away from the excavation.

"A-*ha!*"

Abbie squealed. The flashlight beam wavered. "What is it?" the twins cried.

"Wait a minute, wait a minute," Cap'n Ben muttered in that maddening way people have of raising an alarm and then refusing to tell you why. Jon and Abbie heard rapid scrunching sounds as Cap'n Ben dug at the floor. Flying earth flashed through the white beam.

Some minutes later Cap'n Ben stopped scraping and gouging. The twins heard another *snick!* Then, in the wavering beam of the flashlight, they saw Cap'n Ben lean forward and tug at something. Then he tugged harder. "Get *out* of there, you cussed . . ."

Another few tugs and Cap'n Ben managed to wrench whatever it was loose. He clambered to his feet, grunting slightly. Then he bent down, picked the thing up, crunched toward them in the beam of light, and stopped at the foot of the ladder.

Cap'n Ben was holding up a white bag about two feet long and a foot wide. In the flashlight's beam the faded black letters read:

FIRST ATHOL BANK AND TRUST
EST. 1793

The bag's neck was closed with twine. Whatever was in it filled its bottom third. When Cap'n Ben set the bag down, the twins heard the clink of metal on metal.

Cap'n Ben resumed his search of the cellar floor, Jon playing the flashlight ahead of his feet. "Nothing over heeah . . . this corner's cleeah. . . ."

The twins heard rustling. "Ripped up paper bag. Food wrappings."

Then Cap'n Ben was looking up at the twins. "No sign of anything else down heeyah. But we'll let your dad decide that for himself."

"Oh, yes," Abbie whispered softly.

Cap'n Ben started up the ladder, lumping the bag from rung to rung ahead of him. When his head rose above the floor, Jon clicked off the flashlight.

Cap'n Ben heaved his burden off the top rung of the ladder and dropped it—*chunk!*—onto the worn planks. Then he crawled onto the floor of the old building, levered himself upright, and batted at the knees of his khaki trousers. "Open her up, you two."

The bottom of the bag was filled with coins: silver coins, gold coins, large coins, small coins, irregularly shaped coins, coins with images, coins with holes in them, coins with nicks and pieces cut out of them, coins that looked almost new. . . .

Jon reached in and pulled up a few coins. They looked very old. He let them fall, glittering and clinking, back into the bag.

It really was here. And we figured it out. He thought for a moment. *I wonder when they will come for it. And what they will do when they find* . . .

But aloud Jon said, "Only one bag. And only part full."

"At least the de Parques get something back. And speaking of getting back . . ."

Cap'n Ben looked through the door of the old house. Framed in the doorway, a tiny *Manitou* was lying to the wind under her mizzen. Far out in Butler's Bay a triangle of sail shone brilliant white.

"Jon, go back to the door. Stay well inside so you can't be seen. Abbie, you look out the window over the trapdoor. Can you let that door down by yourself? Tell me if you see anyone around. Don't you fall down that hole, Abbie."

The twins moved quickly over the creaking floor.

The floor shook as the heavy trapdoor banged down. "No one's in sight," Abbie called. "I can see all the way down to the beach on this side."

Jon was standing to one side of the doorway. A light gust eddying through the door ruffled his tousled hair. "Sara just stood up. She's looking this way."

"Probably wondering why we're taking so long. What about boats, Abbie?"

Abbie squinted through the dirty panes. "A few big fishing boats. Standing out to sea."

Staying carefully in the shadows, Jon looked out the door toward the northeast. "Some sailboats, mostly going toward the mainland. And there's a white powerboat." Jon squinted. "Dead in the water."

Yesterday, when they had told Cap'n Ben of their suspicions about

Quarantine Island, they had carefully avoided any mention of the sea skiff or *Thresher*.

Should I tell him now?

Cap'n Ben retrieved the white sack from the edge of the trapdoor. He hefted it. "Jon, take off your windbreaker and zip it up. Now slip your windbreaker over the canvas bag—ay-yup, like that. Now put your hand down through the collar of your coat. Grab the neck of the bag. Ay-yup. Now see if you can lift it."

Jon lifted. The "windbreaker" dragged at his arm and shoulder. He shifted his weight to compensate.

"Well." The wrinkles around Cap'n Ben's eyes deepened. "Have to do. Now for the hard part."

"Well, this isn't . . . 'zackly . . . easy. . . ." Jon said through clenched teeth as he strained to keep his body vertical against the bag's dead weight. Cap'n Ben continued as if he hadn't heard.

"Tote that sack like she's a feather, Jon. Take her right down to the peapod and stow her amidships. Then we're all going to row out to the yawl and get out of here. We'll have that picnic on the way home. Ready, Jon? Ready, Abbie?"

They nodded. Abbie took a deep breath.

Cap'n Ben winked at her. "Okay, let's go."

He and Jon started out the door, Jon trying to swing his windbreaker as if it was a "feather."

As Abbie started after them, a gust of sea air blew a large piece of brown paper out of the shadows by the doorway. It skated across the floorboards, veered toward her, and stopped by her foot. As Abbie bent over, another gust flicked the fragment and it skittered just out of reach. Abbie followed it and reached down. As if teasing her, the piece of brown paper scuttled back toward the shadows inside the door. Abbie dashed after it and pinned it with her sneaker.

It was a piece torn off a brown paper shopping bag. One side was blank. When Abbie turned the fragment over, she found a legend written in thick black ink:

E P O T M 4 H W

"Abbie! Come *on!*"

Abbie folded the brown paper fragment, stuffed it into her dungaree pocket, and ran out the door, then stopped abruptly.

They had forgotten to put the iron bed frame back on top of the trapdoor! She started to scream at the others, but they were halfway down to the beach.

Abbie ran frantically, desperate not to be left behind.

~~~

As *Manitou* swung off toward Butler's Hole before a moderate southerly breeze, Jon looked out of a port cabin light toward the north. Butler's Bay was empty. Puzzled, he climbed the companionway ladder and looked south, then astern toward the beach they had just left.

The white boat had vanished.

Going It Alone

Late Afternoon, Sunday, September 3

Chief Cooper shot to his feet as the glittering stream spilled across his desk. "God of War!" He flipped a switch on his squawk box. "Vernon! Get in heeah!"

While Sergeant Maciel was pounding down the passageway, the chief fired questions at Jon and Cap'n Ben.

"We just looked at the chart, Dad. Quarantine seemed like a good place to start."

"I thought I was humoring them. And there the cussed thing was."

"God of *War!*" the chief roared again. "Vernon! Get on the phone and. . . ."

A very short while later, the Old Town police boat roared out of the harbor, an Old Town patrolman at the helm, the chief, three hastily summoned sheriff's deputies, and one of the island's two state troopers clinging to any handhold they could find.

~~~

A curious sense of anticlimax, almost of defeat, hung over Jon's room.

Miguel was brooding on the cruel fate that perpetually dogged him. "Sunbathing. Shells," he muttered. "And *you* guys discover the bag of coins."

"There's another bag somewhere," Sara reminded him.

"Quarantine's crawling with police," Jon grumbled. "If it's there, they'll find it."

Not a word of praise, Jon thought bitterly. *No "Nice going, kids. How did you ever figure it out?"* Just a lot of bellowing and running around. The police boat had left so quickly he never had a chance to tell Dad about the white boat lurking off Quarantine. The white boat *must* have been *Thresher's* sea skiff. *Well,* Jon thought sourly, *it serves him right. If the other bag was there all the time, the sea skiff's got it by now.*

Abbie was trying to decipher the strange message she had discovered on the floor of the derelict dormitory. The original fragment of brown paper was down at the police station, along with the bag of coins. Abbie had printed the mysterious message in grease pencil on a piece of brown paper torn from a bag in the Coopers' trash bin. She had even crumpled her facsimile like the original.

" 'E P O T M 4 H W,'" Abbie was muttering, " 'E P O T M 4 H W.' The E is right next to the torn edge. The beginning must be on the bag."

Miguel's resentment was fading as the long day waned. "One more day," he yawned. "Then school. Whaddaya say we take the boats out t'morrow?"

Abbie bent over her facsimile. "Is it separate letters?" Abbie liked to think out loud. She didn't expect the others to answer.

Again Abbie crooned the symbols, one by one. "E P O T M 4 H W . . ."

Abbie paused. She studied the black message. "Maybe it's E P O T M 4 H W."

Miguel tried again. "What about a picnic? Over to the cove on Sei? What are the tides tomorrow?"

Sara was trying to coax a weary Jon into helping her figure out where the other bag had been hidden. Jon was lying back on his bunk bed, his hands behind his head, desperately wanting to go to sleep. Abbie, sitting cross-legged on the braided rug, rocked back and forth as she crooned the cryptic message.

Miguel shrugged. Jon kept a copy of the *Pilot's Companion* in the bookshelf over his bunk. Miguel went in search of the familiar yellow book spine.

"Or maybe "E PO TM4 HW,'" Abbie droned. "Is it pronounced 'EEE PO or EH PO?" Then she tried another combination of letters. "Or E POT M4 HW," she said slowly. "Or EH POT M4 HW."

The normally even-tempered Abbie threw her limp piece of paper onto the floor. "Oh, the *hell* with the old stinky *POT!*"

Sara was well into a complex theory about the second bag being somewhere right under their noses when Abbie's angry "*POT!*" rang through the room.

Sara stopped in mid-sentence. She stared for a moment out the dark window. Then she whipped around. "Say that again!" she hissed at Abbie.

Abbie recoiled from Sara's intense blue eyes. "Say *what* again?"

"That message! Say it just the way you did last time!"

"EH POT M4 HW.'" Abbie repeated slowly. She bent and retrieved the piece of brown paper. "Gee, Sara, I've been . . . Hey!" she cried.

"POT!" Sara shouted. "POT!" She brandished the message at the others. "Look! POT! It's right *here!*"

The others goggled at her.

"I'm a dummy!" she cried. "We're all dummies! That's where the other bag is! In the Bend!"

"In the *Bend!*" Abbie repeated. "Whaddaya mean, 'in the Bend'?"

"The Bend in the Graveyard!" Sara leaned toward her friend, her blue eyes blazing. Again Abbie recoiled.

"Ab, what's tomorrow?"

"Monday." Abbie's voice was bewildered. "Labor Day. You know . . . *Gimme* that back!" Abbie cried, snatching the piece of brown paper out of Sara's hand. She stared at it feverishly. Then she threw it in the air. "The pot in the Bend!"

The scrap of paper bag planed down to the chart. Jon picked it up and studied it. "M4," he muttered. "HW. Of *course.*"

"Of course *what?*"

"The *date* tomorrow, Meeg! What *date* is it?"

"Today's the third, so tomorrow's . . . the . . . fourth. . . . Oh!" Miguel exclaimed. "M4 means Monday the fourth!"

"And what does HW always mean?" asked Sara.

"High water!"

"Where's the *Pilot's Companion?*"

Miguel held out the much-thumbed volume. "Hey!" he cried.

"June, July, August, September." Sara tore a page in her haste. "Okay, here we are, Monday, September 4, high water in Butler's Hole: 1:58 a.m. and 2:07 p.m. on the fourth, and again at 2:30 a.m., Tuesday morning, the fifth."

"Graveyard tides are the same time as the Hole's," John said to himself.

"You mean the sea skiff's going to pick up the pot buoy in the Bend tomorrow at high water?"

"That's gotta be it, Meeg." Sara put the *Pilot's Companion* back on its shelf. "They stuck the other bag on the bottom at the Bend with the pot buoy as a marker. But *which* high water? Early morning or afternoon?"

"What difference does it make?" Abbie asked. "We're going to tell Dad about this message."

Jon and Sara turned and looked at her.

Abbie's eyes grew round. *"Aren't* we?"

Miguel's face was solemn as he looked directly at Sara. "We *gotta* tell Chief Cooper."

Sara stared fiercely back. Her voice was tight. "We gave him the cross. We gave him the bag of coins. We gave him the original message. Let *him* figure out what it means." She turned to Jon.

Jon gazed for a moment into Sara's intense blue eyes. She smiled slightly. "Jonno?"

Jon looked down. There were only two ways to go—to Dad and the police, or to the Bend with Sara.

Kids are supposed to tell their folks about stuff like this, Jon thought. Then he remembered that if they told Dad what the message meant, he'd ask them how they knew there was a pot in the Graveyard. . . .

And Sara was right. The second bag was lying on the bottom of the Graveyard, waiting for the thieves to pick it up unless someone else got there first.

They'd been right every step of the way. And now they'd figured out where the second bag was.

But if they *did* go to Dad, would he believe them? Kids' crazy ideas . . . like Miguel's dream . . .

But Miguel's dream had led them to Quarantine Island.

Jon remembered Saturday morning at the police station. Today he was looking into Dad's eyes, on the level. How tall was he going to get? Maybe a lot taller.

Never run away. Running away's the worst thing you can ever do.

Jon looked down at his hands, toughened from a summer of lobstering out on Whale Sound. He closed his hands into fists.

"We've come this far," he said to his hands. He looked up. Sara's blue eyes stared intensely into his. *She's not running away,* he thought. Hard on the heels of that thought came another. *I can't let her go alone. No matter how dangerous it is.*

Jon nodded. "Okay. Let's go for that pot ourselves. Alone."

Again Miguel tried to make the others listen. "That must have been the sea skiff watching us today. Those guys know we found the bag of coins. They'll be pretty mad now, and if they find us pulling up the other bag. . . ."

Sara looked at Miguel.

"I don't want to get anywhere near those guys," he quavered. "Especially that big one. He's weird. It's like he's dead. . . . His eyes are like black holes. . . . Maybe he's a leper. . . ."

"I think we should tell Dad. I don't care if we have to tell him about the Graveyard." Abbie looked at her twin. "If they find us pulling that stuff up . . ."

"They're not *going* to find us!" Sara cried.

"Don't worry, Ab," Jon reassured his twin. "We'll get there first."

"You don't have to go, Miguel. You either, Ab. Jon and I can do this together."

The room became very quiet. Miguel stared down at his feet.

Abbie looked at Jon. "I'll go. If you're going."

"I'm going."

"I don't want to go," Abbie said, "but I will."

Miguel lifted his head and stared directly at Sara.

"I'm going, too. But we better get there plenty early."

"But what'll we say in our float plan?" Abbie wanted to know.

"What we said last time. We're going over to Sei Island. Back no later than five. It's our last day, and we're taking both boats."

Abbie nodded. But she was thinking, *We're still not telling the whole truth. We're still lying.*

Then Abbie thought of something else. This time she spoke her thought.

"If we do find the other bag," she told the others, "we're going to have to tell them where we found it."

The other three didn't seem to hear her. They were staring down at the chart of the Graveyard.

"Now how are we going to do this?" Sara mused.

Rendezvous at the Bend

A few minutes after noon, Labor Day, September 4

Miguel ducked as a big sea smacked the starboard bow. Spray splattered his oilskin hood. *Phoenix* rolled heavily to port.

Lumpy gray seas, their crests flecked with foam, were marching down Whale Sound before a steady easterly breeze. Miguel peered through the mist. A little distance ahead *Loon* was heeling to port as a big sea rose under her. He could just make out the letters on her transom and the silhouette of the loon on the mainsail. "We're gaining," he called.

Loon's mission was to patrol between the southern entrance to the Graveyard and the fairway buoy northeast of East Head. Jon was to blow two blasts on her horn if *Thresher* or the sea skiff appeared.

While *Loon* patrolled, *Phoenix* was to enter the Lower Lane and proceed quickly to the Bend. There Miguel was to snag the red-and-yellow pot buoy with the boat hook. Then Miguel and Sara would raise whatever it was secured to. If it was a lobster pot, they'd drop it. If it was the treasure, they would hoist it aboard.

Whichever it was, they'd be on their way out of the Lane long before high water at 2:07.

"Still on the starboard tack?"

"Still on star . . . Wait a minute." Miguel trained his glasses ahead. "Just swinging into the wind."

Sara peered into the murk to port. They hadn't seen a single vessel since the fog had ambushed them.

"What time is it, Meeg?"

Miguel wiped at his watch. "Twelve-fifteen."

Almost two hours until high water.

~~~

Abbie was steering when *Phoenix* surged by *Loon*. Sheets of spray flew up as the beam seas thumped *Loon's* sides. Jon stopped pumping long enough to wave at Sara and Miguel.

"Ready about!" Abbie's high voice was torn away by the easterly wind.

Loon was too far away for Miguel to hear Abbie's "Hard a-lee," but he saw a tremendous burst of spray as the white sloop plunged head-on into a sea. As *Loon* climbed the next sea, Abbie steered her off the wind. *Loon* heeled over to the steady easterly and reached away from the Graveyard on the southerly leg of her patrol.

Miguel looked to port. With *Loon* astern, nothing lay between *Phoenix* and the Graveyard.

I wish I was home. But who would have helped Sara?

Sara studied the mouth of the Graveyard. Waves trying to run before the wind fell back against themselves as the current battled across their course. She pulled her port tiller line. *Phoenix* rose on the crest of a sea, turned to port, and surfed down the long comber building on the shoal at the southern entrance to the Graveyard.

Saturday's hair-raising excursion into the Graveyard had taught Sara that she had to keep *Phoenix* from broaching—turning sideways and rolling over—in a trough between two seas, or from being swamped by one of the rogue waves heaped up by the easterly wind battling the flood tide roaring through the Lane.

"Miguel!"

Miguel's yellow-clad head snapped around.

"Take your hood off. You can hear me better!"

Miguel threw his hood back.

"Keep your hands on the throttle and the gearshift."

"Okay!"

Miguel sat on the midships thwart, braced himself, and grasped the throttle in his right hand and the gearshift in his left.

"Okay, we don't want to get caught by this wave—"

Miguel twisted the throttle. *Phoenix* leaped ahead of the sea building up astern and ran up the back of the wave just ahead.

"Hold her right on the back of this sea."

The wave passed beneath them and another piled up astern. A rogue wave leaped upward and slopped over the forward gunwales.

Then they were in the lee of Sei Island. Though the flood tide boiled and churned over the rocks at the edge of the narrow channel, the wind no longer buffeted their oilskin hoods and the seas no longer crested. The red pot buoy with its yellow pick-up stick showed clearly against the rocky shore of Minke Island.

"Drop her down some, Miguel." The engine's buzz eased to a low drone.

"There's those three weird rollers." Sara's voice was calm. "I think we had too much power on Saturday. Ease off as we go into that first trough so we don't drive the bow under. Power her up as we climb the wave, then ease her off again."

At the top of the hump of glassy water, the current threw *Phoenix* to starboard, then back to port. Knowing what was coming, Sara neither screamed nor did she try to steer *Phoenix* out of the current's grip. The dory yawed violently through the vortex and dropped her bows into the second trough with a mild thump. Then *Phoenix* was chugging up the Lane on an even keel. They hadn't shipped a drop of water.

"Gee." Miguel looked astern. "That wasn't so bad."

"Rocks are coming in line."

Miguel looked ahead. They were very near the yellow and red pot buoy.

"Stand by." Miguel's hands moved to the throttle and gear shift.

"Back her down a half."

The outboard growled into reverse. *Phoenix* slowed.

"Okay, go forward. I'll handle the engine."

It was a tricky spot. The flood tide running down the Lane toward Whale Sound helped slow the dory, but the wind blowing against her starboard quarter was trying to push her to port as well as move her ahead. Gauging the wind blowing across the flood tide, Sara juggled throttle, gearshift, and rudder as she crabbed the dory toward the pot buoy.

Miguel stood in the bows aiming the heavy wooden boat hook like a harpoon. When *Phoenix*'s bows were over the pot buoy, Miguel lunged and snagged the buoy's pennant, hauled the buoy aboard, threw the boat hook behind him, and began to haul.

"That's it," he panted. "Straight up and down." Miguel hauled at the weight on the end of the pot's anchor line. "It's heavy, but I moved it a little."

Miguel's palms were stinging. He looked down. The line in his hands was spotted with barnacles.

Sara was standing behind him. Her voice was tight. "Okay, Meeg. We'll haul together. Take a turn round the cleat whenever we have to stop. Ready?—Heave! Heave! *Heave!*"

"It's coming," Miguel grunted. "I can feel it dragging on the rocks."

"*Heave! Heave!*"

Phoenix lurched suddenly, swung sideways, and began to drift toward the rocks to the northwest of the Bend.

"*Off* the bottom!" Miguel cried.

Miguel snubbed the pot line on the bow cleat. Sara leaped to the tiller lines. Holding them in her right hand, she moved forward to the engine well and pulled the gearshift. *Phoenix* started to back into the easterly breeze.

Glancing over her shoulder to check how the dory lay to wind and current, Sara put the engine in neutral, cleated the tiller lines, and hurdled the thwarts on her way to the bow. Reaching around her stocky brother, Sara grabbed the pot line below his hands.

"Okay, Miguel, we've got to do it now. Heave—Heave—*Heave!*"

Foot by foot the line came into the dory, dripping with brine, encrusted with barnacles, shedding eel grass and kelp. Suddenly Miguel stopped hauling, snubbed the line on the bow cleat, and leaned over.

"Yellow," he gasped. "Yellow. Not a pot." Then he looked up at Sara. But Sara wasn't behind him.

Pushed by the easterly wind, *Phoenix* had again sagged off toward the rocks to the northwest of the Bend. Back at her steering station, Sara backed the engine and pulled her starboard tiller line. The dory's bows swung to port till they were pointing toward Whale Sound. *Phoenix* was clear of the rocks now and backing slowly against the last of the flood to hold her place in the narrow Bend.

"Okay, Miguel, I'm going to go into neutral. Then we're going to pull that thing on board. Ready?"

Miguel reached down and uncleated the pot's anchor line. He threw the slack behind him so Sara could grab it.

The engine relaxed as it shifted into neutral. Once again Sara lunged across the thwarts and seized the end of the line. "Now!" They swayed forward and hauled. "Heave! . . . Heave!"

They both heard the *swash* of disturbed water as something broke the surface. Again Miguel snubbed the line and they both leaned over the bows.

They were looking at a bulky shape wrapped in yellow oilcloth and lashed with light chain.

Sara looked over her shoulder. The dory was drifting slowly toward the rocks at the northern edge of the Bend.

"Okay, Meeg! *Heave!*"

Together they hauled the heavy weight out of the water and onto the gunwale, the chain grinding into the varnish. Miguel gave a little tug and stepped back. The bundle fell heavily onto the floorboards. As he stared at what they had worked so hard to find, Miguel wiped his stinging palms on his oilskin pants. He didn't see the watery red stains running down his yellow legs.

Phoenix was still drifting sideways toward the rocks. Sara hopped the thwarts crying, "Goose it, Meeg! Goose it!"

Miguel flung himself at the engine, jammed the gearshift into forward, twisted the throttle to the stop, and felt *Phoenix* leap ahead. Then he collapsed on the midships thwart. When he had caught his breath, he unclenched his fists. His stinging palms and fingers were ribboned with crimson.

"We did it, Meeg!" Sara cried to the back of her brother's bowed head. "We got it! Just the way I said we would!" Sara transferred the starboard tiller line to her left hand and stared at her right palm. "You all cut up too, Meeg?"

Miguel held up his palms and nodded. *Phoenix* bounced over the three diminished rollers south of the Bend. Sara barely glanced at them.

"Should we carry the stuff up to the station house ourselves? No! I got a better way." She laughed delightedly. "We'll tell Sergeant Maciel we've got something out in the dory to show the chief. . . ."

Miguel looked forward at the yellow bundle. It reached nearly to the top of the forward thwart. *Better move that thing aft,* he thought. *Bow's digging in.*

Miguel turned and opened his mouth to tell Sara what he was going to do, but nothing came out. He felt all cold inside. For a moment he thought he'd seen something through the mist. Something out in Butler's Bay. Now it was hidden behind Sara's yellow oilskins.

There isn't anything out there, he told himself. *I'm seeing things. . . . If I stay right where I am and don't look . . .*

But the brain has to know the unknown. Despite the voice inside his head warning him not to look, despite the shuddery cold feeling inside him, Miguel leaned to his right and looked past Sara.

A boat was passing the bell buoy out in Butler's Bay, sheets of water fanning to either side of the bow.

Miguel reached for the binoculars and focused the salt-spotted lenses on a white boat turning toward the Upper Lane. A white boat with two figures in it. One of the figures towered over the other. Miguel's stomach crawled again.

Miguel was dimly aware that Sara was speaking to him. Miguel lowered his binoculars. He looked up at his sister. His mouth worked. Then he shook his head. He could not speak.

Sara's eyes widened. She turned her upper body and head. For a moment she remained frozen, looking astern. When she turned and looked down at Miguel, her rose-brown face was pale.

"Oh, Miguel." Sara's eyes closed, then opened. "They came early."

Sara looked to starboard. They were just clearing South Point. She pulled on her starboard tiller line, turning the green dory south-southwest. West Head, invisible in the mist driving across Whale Sound, now lay directly ahead of them. *Phoenix* began to roll heavily in the beam seas.

As *Phoenix* turned to starboard, Miguel lowered the glasses and looked up at Sara. He struggled to speak normally.

"They're slowing down. I don't see their bow wake." Miguel pivoted on the middle thwart and peered through the mist. He could just make out *Loon* ahead and slightly to port. He turned back to Sara. "What are we going to do?"

"I don't think they see us yet. Meeg, show the orange flag. Wait. Don't wave it. Hang it over the port bow."

Miguel put his glasses on the floorboards and leaned over the forward thwart. He plucked the orange distress signal from the forward locker and lashed its lanyards to the bow cleats. Then he moved back to the midships thwart.

At the end of her outbound leg, *Loon* started up into the wind, as if to tack. Then she fell back to her original course. As Sara and Miguel watched, the angle of her sail began to change. *Loon* continued turning until they could see only her varnished stern and a thin curve of brown sail through the mist. The twins had seen the signal. *Loon* was bound for home.

"Check the sea skiff, Meeg!" Sara's voice cracked with tension. She looked astern. With every foot she ran, *Phoenix* was nearing the point where the stunted pines on South Point would shield her from the Bend.

Miguel turned on the midships thwart and tried to hold the glasses steady. Through the driving mist he could just see that the white boat's blunt bow had settled onto the water. It was now moving slowly down the Upper Lane toward the Bend. As Miguel watched, he was praying silently, *Go back! Go back where you came from!*

But as Miguel watched and prayed, the sea skiff's white hull was no longer sliding past the shoreline of Minke Island.

"It's stopping."

Through the glasses Miguel could see the two figures in the boat moving their heads from side to side. Then the smaller of the two figures turned to the larger. Miguel thought he saw the huge helmsman reach forward. The sea skiff started to gather sternway. The smaller figure leaned over the side, then straightened.

As Miguel watched, the sea skiff backed slowly up the Upper Lane toward Butler's Bay. He held his breath. *Were they leaving . . . ?*

No. Miguel saw the white hull stop moving against Minke's rocky shore line. The he saw a small white bow wake. The sea skiff was heading toward them again. Miguel could just see the two crewmen to the right of the pines on South Point. As he watched through his glasses, he saw the smaller of the two figures stiffen and point directly at him. The smaller man ducked down, straightened, and Miguel found himself staring at a pair of binoculars. The binoculars studied Miguel and *Phoenix*. Then the smaller man turned to the giant figure.

The bow of the sea skiff lifted. Sara and Miguel watched helplessly as the white boat roared down the Lower Lane. Once it cleared South Point, the sea skiff turned to starboard and charged at them through the beam seas, throwing spray and solid water to either side as it leaped skyward, then smashed down into the troughs between the waves.

Five minutes later the snarling engine slowed to a deep throaty rumble as the sea skiff came alongside *Phoenix* twenty feet to windward. The giant man with the wolflike face at the wheel glanced once at the green dory as if to gauge his distance, then stared ahead through the heavy mist driving across his course.

The smaller man braced against the starboard side of the sea skiff's steering console was holding a black pistol with a long handle and a short barrel. He peered across at the two yellow-clad figures aboard *Phoenix*, then at the yellow bundle just showing above her forward gunwale. He turned to the giant at the wheel and said something. The giant nodded. The small man turned back to *Phoenix*.

"You rat kids," he snarled across the heaving waves. "You turn west-southwest and follow us. Don't try nothin'!"

The small man pointed his strange-looking pistol at the water between the two boats. Sara was just wondering *Why's he pointing the gun at the water?* when she heard a loud "Brrrrp!" and saw rapid yellow flashes shooting out of the black gun. Little geysers of water leaped up in the turbulent seas. Miguel threw up one elbow and ducked down behind the engine well. Sara flinched but she didn't duck.

They're going to kill us, she thought.

Then the sea skiff pulled ahead and turned slowly to starboard. The small man moved aft and pointed his strange pistol over the huge outboard directly at Miguel and Sara. He jerked the pistol slightly to his left.

Sara pulled her starboard tiller line, and *Phoenix* turned into the wake of the sea skiff.

Twin Decisions

Aboard Loon, *Labor Day afternoon, September 4*

Jon lowered his glasses and looked at his twin, his brown eyes anguished. "It's the sea skiff!"

Abbie looked quickly astern.

"It's right behind them."

Jon reached for the main sheet. "We gotta go back. Jibe, Ab!"

Abbie seized Jon's arm. "Wait a minute. Let's . . ."

"*Jibe!*" Jon glared at his twin and hit her shoulder. "*Jibe!*" He lurched to his feet and reached for the tiller.

Abbie clung to the tiller with both hands. "No, Jon! Jon, *listen* to me!"

Jon forced himself between Abbie and the tiller, thrusting her aside with both arms. Over and over a voice in his head was dinning, *Go back! Go back!* He didn't realize he was shouting the words as he tried to shoulder his smaller twin away from the tiller.

Abbie shot to her feet. The top of her head caught Jon under the chin, snapping his jaws shut. He let go of the tiller and one hand flew to his mouth. "*Quit* it!" Abbie shouted. She placed both hands against Jon's chest and shoved as hard as she could.

Jon staggered backward against the forward coaming. His feet shot out from under him and he sat down hard on the floorboards, banging the back of his head on the coaming as he fell.

"Sit there and *listen* to me!"

Abbie pulled the tiller to windward. When *Loon* was back on course, she looked forward. Jon, still sitting on the floorboards, was rubbing the back of his head with one hand and feeling his jaw with the other.

"We *can't* go back! Miguel held the flag in front of him so the sea skiff couldn't see it. They want us to go for help."

Jon crawled aft, pulled himself up onto the leeward bench, and huddled there, rubbing the back of his head.

"We can't just leave them!" Jon's speech was thick, as if he had bitten his tongue.

"What else can we do? We can't fight those guys. They've probably got a gun. We've *got* to go for help." Abbie glanced at the compass, then corrected course. "What's goin' on now?"

Working his jaw from side to side, Jon leveled his binoculars astern. "The sea skiff's alongside them to windward. . . . Now it's turning down wind. Now Sara's turned the dory downwind." Jon lowered the glasses. "They're headed west."

"Have they spotted us?"

Jon bent down to peer under the boom. "Both guys are looking at the dory." Jon lowered his binoculars and looked at his twin. "It's really hard to tell, but I think one of them has got a gun." *Loon* surged down a quartering sea and rolled to windward. "I wonder if they saw *Loon*."

"Are they looking this way?"

Jon stared through the binoculars at the boats fading into the mist. "Don't seem to be. Still heading west. I can barely see them." He lowered the binoculars. "Must be going for Butler's Hole or Porpoise Island."

Abbie's round face was pale and drawn. Her sodden hair straggled out from under her hood.

"Can you steer, Jonno? I'm pooped."

As they swapped places, Abbie said, "I'm sorry I hurt you, Jonno."

"It's okay." Jon swallowed painfully. "God, Abbie, Sara and Meeg . . ."

"We'll get help, Jonno."

Abbie lay down on the starboard bench, pillowed her head on a sodden life preserver, and shut her eyes.

Jon cocked one leg over the tiller and stared through the glasses at the almost invisible boats. *Still headed west. They must be past Butler's Hole by now. They're going for Porpoise.* He looked at his watch and tried to figure how far they had run since swinging off for Great Whale

Island. Then Jon reached for the chart board and ran his finger along the waters around Porpoise Island until he reached the long line of rocks called "Cow and Calves." Jon studied the chart in snatches, breaking off to scan the sails, the compass, and the water around them as *Loon* headed southwest toward Old Town. His cracked lips tasted salty, and his eyes burned.

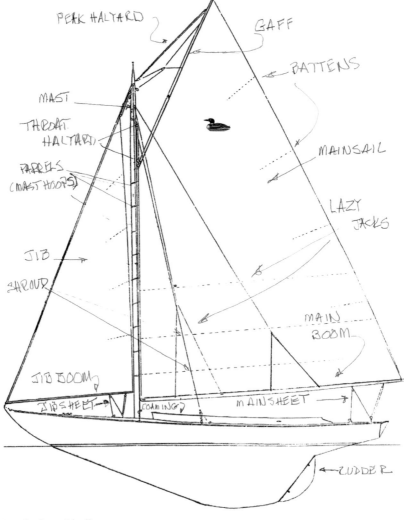

Loon's rig and hull

When Jon next looked to leeward, *Phoenix* and the sea skiff had vanished. *Loon* was alone in the mist on Whale Sound, reaching in a moderating easterly breeze.

Never run away. Never run away.

Jon reached back and uncleated the mainsheet. Pulling the tiller to windward and easing the sheet, Jon put *Loon* dead before the wind on a course roughly parallel to the track *Phoenix* and the sea skiff had been following. As the white sloop began to roll in the leftover seas, Abbie started up.

Jon glanced quickly aloft, then at his twin. "We're going to Porpoise Island, Ab."

Abbie's sleepy eyes widened. *"Porpoise?* Have you gone *soft?"*

"The wind's moderating. It'd take us at least another hour and a half to get to Old Town Harbor. Maybe a lot longer if it goes flat. Once we're there we'll have to explain everything. First they won't believe us. Then they'll have hysterics over the Graveyard stuff. We can't afford to waste that time. We're going to Porpoise Island now."

When Abbie started to protest, Jon shook his head. "You were right back there. Would've been dumb to try to help them. But if we go all the way back to Great Whale, those crooks will have time to . . . to do something. If we move right away, we surprise them. They can't expect anybody to be coming this soon."

Loon rolled sluggishly to windward. Her motion was heavier now, and she was sailing much slower.

"So we're going to do what they don't expect." Jon shoved the chart board toward Abbie and pointed with his left sea boot. "See the southwestern side of the island?" Abbie's yellow hood bent over the chart. "See how deep it is right along the shore? Right before the rocks close in on the northwest corner of the island?" Abbie traced the shoreline with her finger. "We can work in between the shore and the rocks and anchor right here—" Again Jon stabbed at the chart with the toe of his sea boot.

"What do we do then?"

"We'll swim ashore and find Sara and Miguel. When it's dark, we'll get them out of wherever they are. The we'll all go aboard *Loon* and sail back to Great Whale."

The disbelief on Abbie's round face had deepened to horror. She clenched her freckled fists. "Jon! We can't take on that gang."

"We're not going to take them on. We're going to stay away from them. I don't know how we're going to do it, but we're going to rescue Miguel and Sara."

"We can't do it alone!"

"We've got to. Check the searchlight."

Still shaking her head, Abbie extracted the six-cell light from its locker and switched it on. "Working fine."

"Let's eat half a sandwich, have a little water. Save the rest for Sara and Miguel."

"I dunno, Jon." But Abbie bent to pull the cooler out from under the foredeck.

Jon checked his watch: 3:10. Over the bow he could just make out the red flashes of West Head light. When he looked astern, he caught the briefest glimpse of the Whale Sound fairway buoy before the mist obscured it.

After they had eaten and swallowed some water, and used a very little more water to wash their smarting eyes, they estimated their position and the distance to the southwest corner of Porpoise Island, then their speed. Abbie moved her lips as she silently worked out the rate-time-distance formula Commander Selph had taught the twins and Sara.

"We ought to be close to Porpoise by 4:15." She thought for a moment. "Maybe more like 4:30."

"Before nightfall." Jon looked into the driving mist. "The visibility's real poor now. By 4:30 it'll be worse. When's sunset?"

"About 7."

"What's the forecast again?"

"Clearing. Wind's goin' to go northwest."

"We'll let the tide set us south. Then we'll jibe and work our way in nice and quiet."

"Quiet," Abbie said. "Yeah." She dropped to her hands and knees. "I'm going to take the chain off the anchor line," she said as she crawled under the foredeck. "So they won't hear us when we put the hook over."

Prisoners Aboard *Thresher*

Late Afternoon, Labor Day, September 4

Miguel raised *Phoenix*'s propeller shaft clear of the bottom as the dory slid onto the gravelly shingle. The heavier sea skiff, her huge engine already tilted, crunched to a stop close to port. Three horn blasts sent seagulls crying aloft.

The small man in the sea skiff pointed his black pistol at Sara and snarled, "Girl. Sit down. Hands on knees. Boy. You, too."

Sara pulled her yellow hood over her head and sank slowly onto the after thwart, her hands on her knees. The salt on her oilskins stung her lacerated palms and fingers. As if totally cowed, Sara bent forward slightly and lowered her head. Then, shielded by her hood and carefully moving her eyes, not her head, Sara sized up her surroundings.

To her left the small man, his pistol now dangling from his right hand, was standing between the sea skiff's broad starboard deck and her steering console, a flimsy plywood structure rather like a lectern with a yellowing plastic wind screen fastened to its forward edge. Some scales of yellow varnish still clung to the weathered wood. The steering wheel was mounted on the after side of the console. The engine controls were fastened to the starboard side of the console's top, in the center of which sat a small domed compass. The hulking man was sitting on a backless wooden bench just aft of the console, one hand on the sea skiff's steering wheel.

On the far side of the sea skiff Sara could see *Thresher* alongside a rickety-looking dock, her stern to the shore and her bow pointed toward the entrance to the cove. Swiveling her eyes to the right, Sara could see the three shacks she had spotted when they entered the cove. They were huddled beneath the dunes fifty yards above the high tide line. Farther to her right a rocky shore rose to low sand hills covered with scrubby vegetation. The humid air stank of rotting fish and seaweed.

When Sara swiveled her eyes back to her left, the small man and the hulking figure were staring at her. The small man gestured toward *Phoenix*'s bow with his pistol. Sara looked quickly at Miguel's back and tried to sit motionless.

~~~

Somewhere to her right and above her, Sara heard a screen door bang. Keeping her head still, Sara swiveled her eyes to the right and saw two familiar figures emerge from the largest of the three tumbledown shacks and start down the weedy slope—the enormously fat man and the *Thresher*'s captain, who was still wearing the leather vest over his bare chest. Sara dropped her eyes and waited.

Loud footsteps crunched closer and closer. Then they stopped. Sara instinctively raised her head, then waited apprehensively for a curt order from the small man. But he was silent.

The captain and his mountainous henchman had stopped at the dory's bow. The captain glanced at the yellow bundle lying on the floorboards, then at Miguel slumped on the forward thwart, then at Sara sitting stiffly on the stern thwart and staring at him. He turned sharply toward the sea skiff. Sara saw the small man flinch back against the steering console.

"Cap'n Craven," the small man said, the words tumbling over each other, "just listen. Okay? Just lemme tell you. . . . We got to the Graveyard plenty early, just like you said, but the marker was gone. Then we spotted this boat out in the Sound. Them two kids there, they had the stuff. Same ones we saw over at Quarantine. They was alone this time. Orcutt and me, we thought maybe we'd better—"

"—bring 'em here for me to deal with." Craven stared expressionlessly at the small man, then at his gigantic mate. "Turco, I dunno about you and Orcutt. Been me, I woulda taken the stuff and. . . ."

Craven turned and fixed his eyes on Sara.

They're the color of water. The color of nothing.

Craven's pale gray eyes roamed across Sara's face, then down her glistening yellow form. He bared crooked, yellow teeth. "Well," he said slowly. "Maybe you done right. . . ."

Craven walked toward Sara, his boots crunching slowly on the wet gravel. As he got closer, Sara saw that the stain on his right arm was a tattoo of the circling shark on the *Thresher*'s stern. Several days' stubble darkened his sallow cheeks. She tried to keep her face blank as Craven neared. Everything inside her was shrinking.

"One bag of coins not enough for you, Bright Eyes?"

Craven cocked his head and waited.

"Nothin' to say, Bright Eyes?" Craven shrugged. "Don't matter."

Craven jerked his head toward the others behind him. "Orcutt and Turco saw you at Quarantine Island yesterday. Layin' out in the sun. You got yourself a real nice tan, didn't you, Bright Eyes? While them others found the bag of coins."

Sara tried again to look away. Her lips were dry. She hoped her bulky oilskins hid the trembling.

His eyes still fixed on Sara, Craven spoke over his shoulder. "When we're under way, Bright Eyes is gonna tell us how they knew the rest of the stuff was in the Graveyard. And where Ben Pease and them other kids is. Right, Bright Eyes? Ain't cha?"

Craven walked slowly down the dory's starboard side until he towered above Sara, his scarred face blotting out the sky. She clenched her teeth to choke back a sob. "You gonna tell us all about that. Ain't cha?"

Craven studied Sara's upturned face. He seemed to see into her numbness, to hear her choked-back sobs.

Craven raised a battered hand. Sara closed her eyes as the broken fingernails moved slowly toward her face. She felt her hood flicked backward off her head. When rough fingertips scraped across her right cheek, Sara's eyes shot open. She gasped and shot across the thwart until her back was jammed against the port gunwale, raising her right hand to her cheek as if she'd been hit. Sara stared at Craven, waiting.

Craven dropped his hand but he held her eyes with his. "Listen, Bright Eyes. This ain't some kids' game. You're gonna tell us everything, and then we're gonna decide what to do with you. And the brat there. Plenty of time for that, Bright Eyes. On the way out."

Craven straightened. "Orcutt. Turco. Lock 'em in the after cabin. Come on, Packy."

Then Craven tapped the dory's forward gunwale with his right hand. "And this here," he said looking at the two in the sea skiff, still tapping the dory's gunwale. Sara saw Craven flick his right hand across his throat. Out of the corner of her eye she thought she saw Turco nod.

Craven looked back at Sara and winked. "See you later, Bright Eyes."

Glancing briefly at the yellow form huddled on the forward thwart, Craven strode up the beach, his sea boots crunching on the shingle. Packy waddled in his wake, rolls of fat jiggling under his shirt.

Miguel and Sara were yanked out of the dory, hustled up the rickety dock, shoved across the scarred deck, and locked in the aftermost of two small cabins abaft *Thresher*'s wheelhouse. The porthole in the starboard-side cabin's door looked directly onto the low neck of sand at the eastern edge of the cove.

As Orcutt's and Turco's bootsteps faded down the deck, Sara tiptoed to the door and eased the handle downward. It moved smoothly, but the door wouldn't budge, even when she leaned against it. Sara bent and looked through the keyhole. She couldn't see a thing.

Sara had heard the key turn but not the familiar scrape and rattle it would have made if it had been withdrawn.

Orcutt and Turco must have left the key in the lock.

While Miguel struggled out of his soaked oilskins, Sara examined their prison. The small deadlight in the door was made of thick, scratched plastic. The only other source of light was two deadlights let into the cabin's starboard bulkhead—fixed circles of plastic you could not open. Sara looked up—no hatches led out through the overhead. She couldn't see a ventilator opening anywhere. The only way out was the cabin's locked door.

When Sara finished her inspection, Miguel was lying on one of the two wooden bunks wrapped in a tattered quilt. His eyes were shut.

Sara suddenly felt exhausted, more tired than she thought was possible. She sat on the other wooden berth, shucked off her oilskins, then sank back onto the moldy pillow. She squeezed her eyelids tight shut, trying to blot out Craven's colorless eyes and the wolfish Orcutt's dead face. Tried not to feel the rasp of Craven's fingers on her cheek. She thought of Turco's black pistol. Of Orcutt licking his thin lips.

Sara saw again the long row of white stepping-stones, the trail of black footprints following her as she marched up the path toward the future.

I wish I could walk back down the calendar, back to yesterday, to last week. She buried her face in the moldy pillow.

Don't cry now, *you jerk. Too late for that.*

But the tears kept oozing. *If only Miguel hadn't kicked that clump of rockweed. If only she had listened to him.* Sara remembered his frightened eyes and his quavery voice. *"We gotta tell Chief Cooper."*

Then Sara heard her own voice: *"We gave him the cross. We gave him the bag of coins. We gave him the original message. He can figure out what it means."*

Sara heard herself sneering, You *don't have to go, Miguel.* But what choice had she left him? What else could he say but, *"I'm going too. . . . But we better get there plenty early."*

Sara heard another voice saying, "Think of the consequences."

It's all because of me we're here. If Miguel gets hurt, it will be all my fault.

Sara hugged her pillow with both arms. *Mom. Dad.*

Then she slept.

Rescue

Late Afternoon–Early Evening, Labor Day, September 4

The twins, their clothes clammy inside their oilskins, were lying slightly below the crest of the dunes that rose above the beach where *Loon* was anchored.

Jon looked over his shoulder. In the misty twilight he could barely make out *Loon*'s white hull and furled sails as she swung to her anchor just off the steep-to shore. Jon was counting on that light-colored boulder half-buried in the sand to guide them back to her once the light had gone.

Jon wriggled his way up the dune until he was peering down through a thicket of beach plum and gorse that grew just below the crest on the cove side of the dunes. Abbie wriggled up after him and settled to his right.

The three weathered shacks below the twins were perched well above the gravelly southwest shore of Porpoise Island's nearly circular cove. To their right a rickety dock straggled out from the rocky beach on the east side of the cove. The *Thresher* was secured to the east side of the dock, her stern to the beach and her bow pointed northwest. The sea skiff was beached on the west side of the dock.

Jon sniffed. The dank easterly wind ruffling their matted hair carried the sour odors of dried seaweed and rotting fish. Jon scanned the dismal scene. *Where's Phoenix?* he suddenly wondered.

Abbie had also been examining the circular cove. "Where's *Phoenix?*" she whispered.

The twins carefully scanned the entire cove. The little green dory was nowhere in sight.

Jon shook his head. "No idea. Maybe on the far side of *Thresher?*" he offered hopefully.

During the next half hour the twins saw the fat man carry duffel bags and boxes aboard *Thresher.* He and the huge man used *Thresher's* jib crane to hoist three fifty-gallon drums from the dock onto the boat deck and lashed them to ringbolts set into the deck and the after end of the wheelhouse. When the lashings were secure, Orcutt and Packy walked down the dock and climbed the sandy path to the three shacks. The twins heard the door of the middle shack bang.

"They must be getting ready to leave," Jon whispered. Abbie nodded. "Sara'n Miguel must be locked up on the *Thresher.* But listen . . . maybe they'll leave 'em behind. . . ."

Abbie shook her head slowly. "They won't. Sara'n Meeg know those guys are the burglars. And now they're kidnappers."

Then Jon felt Abbie's elbow nudge his. He turned and looked into his twin's brown eyes.

"You like Sara, don't you, Jon." It wasn't a question.

Jon looked at his twin, then quickly looked away at *Thresher* while he tried to think what to say. But there was no point in pretending to Abbie.

"Yeah. Yeah, I guess I do. I'm sorry, Ab."

Abbie grinned. "What are you sorry for? Sara's nice. Just bossy right now. It's okay. She'll get better. And we'll always be twins."

Despite his sodden clothes and the dank wind ruffling his matted hair, Jon's ears felt hot. He tried to think of something to say, but Abbie had turned back to study the three shacks.

The twins watched for five more minutes. No one came out of the middle shack. Jon could see into *Thresher's* wheelhouse through the port and after windows. There was no movement within.

Jon put his head next to Abbie's. "We're going to slide back down the dunes to the beach, then run around to the east end of these dunes. We'll be real near *Thresher* there, and those guys won't be able to see us. Ready?"

Jon took one last look to his right. The steep dunes lost height as they curved to the east until they merged into the beach some ten yards southeast of *Thresher's* dock. Until the twins reached that point, the dunes would shield them from the shacks. When they left the dunes for the open beach and ran the last ten yards toward the dock, their only cover would be *Thresher*'s black hull. They would be completely exposed, Jon saw, as they ran along the dock and jumped aboard *Thresher*. Once they were aboard *Thresher*, the starboard side of the wheelhouse would cover them.

The twins crawled backward until they were below the crest of the dunes. Then they slid down the steep slope in an avalanche of damp sand and ran. When the crests of the dunes were barely five feet above the beach, Jon grabbed Abbie's arm. The gasping twins crouched and listened.

After they had caught their breath, Abbie slowly stood until, half crouched, she could see just over the dunes. She was looking at the top of *Thresher*'s mast. With infinite caution, Abbie rose her remaining two inches and found herself looking at the open-mouthed shark on *Thresher*'s transom and the three fifty-gallon drums lashed abaft *Thresher*'s wheelhouse. She could make out the bow of the sea skiff beached on the far side of the dock. No one was visible. The only sounds were the occasional cry of a seagull and the wind ruffling the dune grass. Abbie dropped back next to Jon.

"Ready?"

Abbie nodded.

The twins scuttled the last few feet on hands and knees and lay flat on the damp sand. The light was fading fast.

Jon checked his watch. "Dark in an hour. Let's go."

~~~

The Coopers' cuckoo clock was chirping six o'clock as Marie Selph hung her glistening yellow coat on the back of the kitchen door. "Alan just called. A thirty-six-footer is going to patrol between West Head and Sei Island. But they'll probably show up any minute."

She and Betty Cooper looked out the curved kitchen window. They could just make out *Loon*'s mooring buoy fifty yards off the beach. As they watched, a curtain of fog blew across the dunes. The mooring buoy vanished. "The forecast didn't say anything about fog," Marie Selph said sadly.

At seven o'clock all four parents were at the Coast Guard Station. The children's float plan lay on Commander Selph's desk.

Tom Cooper peered into the thick night. "*Loon* doesn't have running lights," he muttered to himself.

A knock at the open door, then a sailor stuck his head inside. "Beg pardon, Captain. The 200 boat reports no boats between here and Sei. But it's pretty thick."

Commander Selph glanced at the clock. Then he looked at the float plan—a simple message in Abbie's round handwriting answering the familiar questions: Who was going, where they were going, which boats they would take, assurance that they had checked the weather and that they'd put gas, life preservers, and food aboard. Navigational gear and ground tackle always stayed aboard. Finally, at the bottom, the Estimated Time of Departure—they all knew the children had left before eleven that morning—and Estimated Time of Arrival back home: 5 P.M.

It was now 7:20 P.M. Alan Selph picked up his phone.

"XO, I want you to keep the 200 boat patrolling. If they haven't sighted the kids by twenty hundred hours, *Schoodic Head* will go out. I'll go aboard *Schoodic*. You're in command here until I get back. Bring *Sankaty* to stand by in case we have distress calls. At twenty-one hundred, you can recall the 200 boat. That's it."

Commander Selph was using the military's twenty-four-hour system of keeping time. Twenty hundred (2000) hours was 8 p.m. to civilians. After noon, you simply add twelve to each hour: one P.M. becomes thirteen hundred hours to the military, and so on.

Alan Selph rose. His eyes were tired, but he smiled as he looked from his wife to Betty Cooper to Tom Cooper. "Gotta go. I'll be back when I'm back." He grabbed his baseball cap and was gone.

The Coopers and Marie Selph watched as sailors began moving about the deck of the eighty-three-footer. The deep-throated rumbling of powerful engines filled the air. They saw Alan Selph cross the open space in front of the Coast Guard Station and haul himself aboard *Schoodic*.

"We'd best go back to the house," Tom Cooper said. "Marie, please come with us."

Marie Selph nodded silently. Betty Cooper put an arm around her friend's shoulder and they started for the door.

It was 7:45.

~~~

A bewildered, sleep-sodden Sara found herself staring at a completely unfamiliar discolored white ceiling. *Where* am *I?*

Then she felt the frayed quilt and smelled the mildewed pillow.

Sara rolled over and looked at the porthole in the locked door. The sky was dark gray. She turned her head. In the waning twilight Sara could just make out a hand and a foot protruding from Miguel's quilt. As she started to close her eyes, she thought she heard something. Sara propped herself on her elbows and listened.

Nothing.

Sara was about to settle back onto the mildewed pillow when she froze and held her breath.

Faint scraping noises? She listened intently. Yes!

The scraping noises stopped, then started. Nearer this time. Like someone shuffling across a sandy floor. Then they stopped again.

Sara rolled to her left so that she could see her watch. Almost 7.

Lying on her side motionless, Sara listened hard.

Nothing. She held her breath.

Still nothing.

Then Sara sat bolt upright. There! The faint scraping footsteps had started again.

Sara sat motionless, her heart thundering. These were not the arrogant, thumping boots of Orcutt and Turco.

The faint, scraping footsteps started again. They seemed to be on the starboard deck and coming nearer. *Mom has a light walk. . . .*

Sara slid off her bunk and pressed her face against the porthole, trying to see aft.

The light footsteps slid closer and closer, then stopped. A pale shape appeared suddenly in the porthole, and two eyes looked directly into hers.

Sara started backward. She heard a muffled "Sara!" and saw Abbie clap her hand across her mouth and stare desperately aft, her rigid profile framed in the porthole. Then Abbie's head disappeared.

Sara heard the familiar scrape and rattle. The door inched open, and Abbie darted into the cabin, threw her arms around Sara, and hugged as hard as she could.

Sara hugged back, thinking *She's all sandy.*

Another faint rattle and Jon slipped through the door, the key in his hand. He closed the door quietly. Sara tore herself from Abbie's sturdy grasp and threw her arms around Jon's neck. She felt his arms close about her and his cold face press against hers.

"You were s'pose to go back to Great Whale," she whispered in his ear. Then she kissed the ear.

"Would've taken too long." Jon dropped his arms. "Why are you spitting?"

"Your ear's all sandy."

Jon swiped at his sandy ear as he leaned over Miguel's bunk and shook the mound under the quilt. "Let's go, Miguel."

Miguel started up, his eyes wide. Jon held his hand over Miguel's mouth. "You awake?"

Miguel nodded. Jon took his hand away. Miguel rolled off the bunk and threw his arms around Jon's waist.

"Jon." The older boy looked down. "They're leaving at nine! They're going to take us with them!"

Jon looked at his watch. "After seven. Roll your oilskins up and stick 'em in your boots. Okay, me first, then Miguel, then Sara. Ab, here's the key. Lock the door. Bring the key with you."

Jon eased the door open and peered around its frame, then beckoned. "Let's go!"

The others crept after him along the *Thresher*'s worn deck.

Near the after end of the cabin house Jon gestured backward with his opened hand. The others stopped and crouched.

Jon crawled ahead until he could peer around the cabin house. Then he eased back.

"They're coming out of the shack," he whispered. "Squeeze between the life lines and slide down the tail of that dock line. Abbie first, then Sara, Miguel, and me."

A faint splash and Abbie was paddling quietly toward the beach. Sara gasped as she sank into the cold, black water. Miguel followed so quickly he almost landed on her head.

When she was clear of the water, Abbie ran to the end of the dunes and vanished. Sara and Miguel waded out of the water with their bundles of foul-weather gear and ran after her. Jon was right on their heels. Shielded by the dunes, the four friends clutched each other.

"Your toe okay, Meeg?" Jon whispered.

Miguel waggled it experimentally, then nodded. His teeth were chattering such that he could not speak.

"Let's go!"

Jon pelted down the beach, the others panting along behind him. Once Miguel tripped and fell headlong with a soft grunt. Before Sara could turn, he was up and running again.

After fifty yards of wild flight, the four friends steadied to an even jog, no longer running away from something but moving purposefully toward safety.

Then Jon stopped abruptly and held up his arms. Sara and Abbie panted up beside him. Miguel, who had been jogging head down, cannoned into Abbie and knocked her flat in the soft sand.

"Miguel!" Abbie staggered to her feet. "You tryin' to kill me?"

"I didn't see you stop!" The indignant Miguel was on his hands and knees feeling around for his bundles. "It's dark, for cripes sake! What are you stoppin' for, anyways? Are we supposed to be 'scapin' or what?"

"Will you two shut *up*! We're here!"

Jon crept quietly away from the foot of the dunes. Then he turned and ran his eye the length of the dunes. Nothing showed against the dark sky. He heard only the dying breeze rustling the dune grass. He turned toward the boulder near the water's edge. For a moment he felt a black despair as he searched the dark waters. Then he just made out *Loon*, still right where he and Abbie had left her, sailing quietly back and forth at her anchor.

"Come on," he hissed. The four friends ran the ten yards from the rock to where *Loon* waited for them.

As he waded into the water, Jon felt a puff of air on his right cheek—his right, not his left. He looked up. The cloudy sky was peppered here and there with silver. Looking to the south, he could clearly see the distant flash of the lightship marking the entrances to Whale Sound and Butler's Bay.

Clouds are breaking up, Jon thought. *Mist's gone. Cold front's coming through.*

A few quick strokes and *Loon* towered over them. Abbie grabbed the main sheet with both hands and pulled herself up until her feet could reach the swimming steps bolted to the transom. Treading water and holding onto the gunwale with one hand, Jon turned. Sara and Miguel were holding their bundles of foul-weather gear high as they half-waded, half-swam toward him.

Porpoise Island

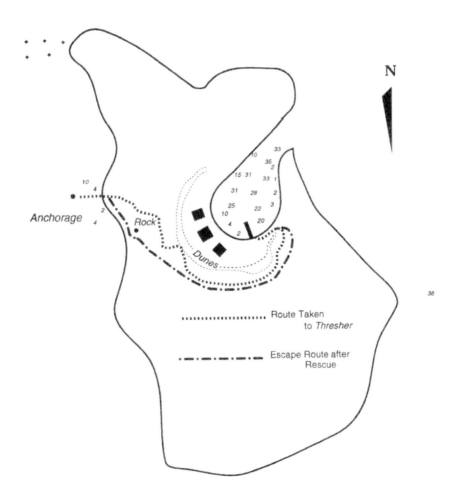

Anchorage

Rock

Dunes

N

·················· Route Taken
to *Thresher*

· — · — · — · — · Escape Route after
Rescue

Still holding the gunwale, Jon lofted Miguel's bundles into *Loon*'s cockpit. "Quick," he gasped. "Go on up. Breeze's gone northwest." He boosted the younger boy up until he could grab the main sheet and then get his good foot on the lower swimming step. Sara followed Miguel.

Once aboard, Jon said, "Steer, Abbie. Sara—" Jon pressed his knife into Sara's cold hand—"cut the anchor line when the main's up."

Sara looked up at him. Good sailors *never* leave their anchors behind.

"Do it! It's quicker. And quieter."

Jon hoisted the mainsail, wincing as the sheaves whined and the wooden mast hoops rattled up the mast. Never again, Jon promised himself, would he fail to oil *Loon*'s turning blocks.

As Jon cleated the throat halyard, the bitter end of the severed anchor line slithered across the deck and disappeared through the chock. No longer tethered, *Loon* swung slowly to starboard. Jon hoisted the peak, cleated its halyard, and winced again at the screeching blocks when Abbie paid out the mainsheet. As Miguel hoisted the jib, *Loon* turned faster toward the southeast.

"Ab, can you see the shoreline?"

Abbie turned and looked to port. "Uh . . . Yeah! I can see the kelp at the edge of the beach."

"Follow the contour of the beach but keep a little off. When the shore turns east, we can, too."

Loon was running smoothly before the freshening nor'wester. The calm water chuckled comfortably along her side. A fresh puff heeled *Loon* to starboard. She began to sail faster. Jon felt his way aft and sank down on the port bench beside Abbie.

"No moon, Jon."

"Thank God," he whispered. He looked up. Hastened by the strengthening northwest wind, the remaining clouds were scudding fast to the east, leaving more and more stars in their wake.

Jon held up his left wrist and tried to read the time. In the starlight it looked like eight o'clock, but was his watch still running? The thieves said they'd be leaving at nine. Had they already tried to open the locked cabin and found the captives missing? If they hadn't, they would soon. What would they do then? Look for them? Or just run for it?

"Check the shoreline, Jon."

There was more open water now between them and the shore. The beach had almost vanished. Jon looked over the port bow. In the distance he thought he saw a flashing red light. He waited. There it was again.

"Ab," Jon whispered. Then, in his normal voice, "What am I whispering for? They can't hear us. Ab, look over the port bow. See anything?"

Abbie turned her head and remained motionless, straining to see in the dark. Then she shook her head.

"Nothin'. What am I—There! Just saw a flash." She held motionless. "Yeah! Red flash."

"I'm bettin' that's West Head," Jon said. 'Too far away to see steady. Steer in that direction. We'll pick it up in a while."

"Oh, *yes!*" Abbie breathed.

"Head right for it when you see it. It should flash every four seconds."

The turning blocks rattled as Jon trimmed the main. *Loon* heeled as her bow came up and pointed directly at where Abbie thought she'd seen the dim red light. She could feel the muscles of her shoulders and arms begin to relax. "Don't let me fall asleep, Jonno."

"I'm going to sleep for two years." Jon looked astern at the black bulk of Porpoise Island. "After we get home."

A cold puff heeled *Loon* to starboard. Sara and Miguel pulled on their wet oilskins and boots, then stretched out side by side on the floorboards, with soggy life preservers for pillows.

Loon was well into Whale Sound now. Her bows lifted and fell in the growing swell. Another fresh gust heeled the sloop to starboard. The quarter wake sparkled with phosphorescence.

Jon looked up. The freshening nor'wester had cleared away all but a few patches of cloud. The peppering of stars he had glimpsed earlier was now a scintillating canopy of incandescence flung across the dark bowl of the sky from zenith to horizon all around the compass.

Jon tried to imagine what they looked like from up there—a thin trail of sparkles creeping across the black sea.

The Battle with the Sea Skiff

Late Evening, Labor Day, September 4

Anodding Jon jerked awake, remembered where he was, rubbed his stinging eyes, and looked over the port bow. The intermittent red light he thought was West Head was now flashing steadily, directly on *Loon*'s plunging bow. He counted the seconds between flashes: *one—two—three—four!*

"West Head for sure," he whispered to Abbie.

"Dead on it," she whispered back.

Jon looked to windward. No lights to the northwest. He peered under the boom. Broad on the starboard quarter, Jon could make out the faint red, green, and white lights of fishing boats on Luce Shoal.

Jon looked astern. After a long moment he nudged Abbie, held his finger to her lips, and whispered, "Look back at Porpoise."

Abbie turned, looked, then caught her breath.

Little points of light were crawling across the dark hump of Porpoise Island. Two were up high—on the dunes, Abbie guessed. Two other lights were moving about lower down and to the left.

"Look at those lower lights," Jon whispered. "They'll probably find our tracks in the sand. They'll know Miguel and Sara escaped by boat. But they won't know what kind of boat and where it went."

"Maybe they saw *Loon* this afternoon."

The twins sat quietly for a moment. "We're slow," Jon murmured. "But we're showing no lights. There's no moon. Maybe they'll see our sails against the stars."

"They may see the hull, too."

"Maybe they won't bother with us. They've got their loot. They may just leave and be done with it."

"They'd never let us go. We can prove they're thieves—and kidnappers. Pirates even."

"Well, let's not make it easy for them." Jon crawled forward and reached over Sara's curled-up yellow form for the spinnaker bag and its pole.

The thrashing of the spinnaker woke Sara. She sat up and rubbed her eyes. Miguel didn't stir. Jon cleated the halyard, trimmed the guy aft, and the spinnaker filled with a loud *clap*! *Loon* heeled to starboard and surged ahead, her quarter wake much louder now and filled with phosphorescence.

Sara sank back out of the wind. Jon braced both feet against the leeward bench and looked at the spinnaker's luff, then at West Head's red flashes, then back at the spinnaker. *Godfrey, I'm cold*, he thought. *I've never been this cold.*

~~~

Jon had dozed off again when Abbie nudged him. "I hear engines." She was looking astern. "Two sets. One sounds like the sea skiff. Over there." Abbie pointed over the starboard quarter toward the southwest and the entrance to Whale Sound. "Other engines are deeper." Abbie jerked her head toward the northeast. "To windward."

Jon listened a moment. "Those engine noises are separating."

Sara sat up again. "I been thinking. They know we're trying to get back to Great Whale. I bet the *Thresher*'s going to block the middle of the sound. The sea skiff will go southwest, then she'll turn back this way and try to trap us between them."

Now Miguel sat up. His voice was steady, unafraid. "Think they'll find us?"

"We're little," Jon said. "We're hard to see. We're going pretty fast. And they're almost out of time."

"How come?"

"The Coasties have *got* to be coming out soon. Soon's we see their lights, Miguel's going to pop off an S-O-S."

"Yeah!" Miguel said. "Yeah! S-O-S! I know that signal! Where's the searchlight?" He started scrabbling in the starboard locker.

"We've got to watch in all directions," Jon warned the others.

Sara dumped her life preserver forward of the port bench and knelt on it, her arms propped on the coaming. "I'll take the weather side."

Jon shifted across the cockpit to the starboard bench. "I'll take the leeward side."

"I'll stay on the helm and trim the main." Abbie's voice was strong. "Just tell me where to steer."

Miguel knelt on the floorboards at the forward end of the cockpit, his arms resting on the coaming—just as they had rested on his window sill a few nights before, Miguel remembered—so long ago.

~~~

"I can't hear *Thresher* anymore."

Jon was kneeling forward of the starboard bench, his back to Sara, looking intently to the southwest. He didn't turn. "I can't hear the sea skiff either. No lights except for fishing boats on Luce Shoal."

"I can see West Head real clear," called the forward lookout. "Hey! I got the green flasher! More to port!"

"Steer for the flasher," Jon told Abbie. The green flasher would help *Loon* clear the wilderness of rocks off West Head called "The Brick Pile."

When Abbie hardened up a few degrees, the spinnaker broke with a sharp *clap*. Jon reached for the sheet, but the sail filled itself and *Loon* surged ahead.

For a while the tired, shivering crew heard only the sigh of the wind and the hiss of the stern wake as the little white sloop rode the northwest wind toward Great Whale Island. Another gust, another *clap!* and *Loon* slid down a white-capped sea in a hissing smother of sparkling foam. Abbie reached over the cockpit coaming and patted *Loon*'s side. "Go, little *Loon*, go, baby!" she whispered.

The sea ran out from under *Loon*. Another fresh gust and again the spinnaker broke—two sharp *cracks*. *Loon*'s hull shook.

"Jon, the wind's heading us."

"You can come off a little. Flood's just begun. The current will set us up toward the flasher."

"*Thresher's* engines!" the forward lookout cried suddenly. "Going real fast!"

They could all hear the distant bellow of big diesels. Jon peered to windward. Were the bellowing engines fading slightly?

Then Jon spun.

At first there was only the menacing snarl of an enormous engine out in the night somewhere astern of them. Then, all of a sudden, there was the sea skiff. Jon rubbed his grainy eyes and looked again. He couldn't wish away the white hull, or the hollow booming of the blunt bows pounding the waves.

Jon felt empty. He was shivering cold, drained of strength, drained of ideas, drained of energy. He slumped against the coaming, tried to think, and couldn't. He didn't know what to do. They were trapped.

Then he felt a shoulder against his. "Jon?"

He turned. Sara's arm went around his shoulders. "You came and got us," she whispered into the sandy ear. "We almost made it."

Almost made it . . . Never run away . . .

Jon forgot he was shivering cold, that he and his friends were hopelessly trapped, that the thieves in that white boat so close behind them had at least one gun.

Jon pushed away from Sara and stood. "Those—!" he said, using a short and very regrettable word. "Those—!" he said again. "Guys! Find something! We're gonna fight those—!" He looked frantically around the cockpit.

"Fight!" Miguel echoed. "Yeah! We're going to *fight!*"

Miguel dove for the locker under the starboard bench, snapped down the hatch, and dragged out the sounding lead and the lead line. "Yeah! We're going to *fight* those—!" If Jon could say it, so could he!

Miguel was holding an old-fashioned sounding lead and its line. The lead was a heavy, truncated, footlong cylinder of lead with a concave depression in its wide bottom and an eye at its narrower top to which the sounding line was attached. Leather tags and cloth pieces were fixed at intervals in the line's strands. To measure the water's depth, a seaman would cast the lead well ahead, pulling in the line as the boat caught up with the lead. When the line was straight up and down, the leadsman would read the depth—or feel the depth at night—and call it back to the navigator.

Loon's lead would not be sounding tonight.

Jon crawled forward and seized the little grapnel they used to anchor on a rocky bottom. This metal shaft, with five or six curved arms ending in sharp points, was attached at the other end to a long line. During the days of fighting sail, sailors would hurl grapnels aboard an enemy ship and lash the two vessels together. Then the hand-to-hand fighting would begin.

Jon and Miguel worked feverishly in the dark to ensure that their lines were free of snarls and would uncoil smoothly when they hurled the lead line and the grapnel. Jon dangled the grapnel by its line from his right hand. His left held a few fathoms of coiled line that he would pay out after he threw the grapnel at the sea skiff.

Miguel, standing forward of Jon, was not only left-footed; he was left-handed as well. He dangled the sounding lead by its line from his left hand, the spare coils held in his right. The he stared over the starboard quarter at the grim white shape cutting across their wake.

"So what are we going to do, Jon?" He swung his lead in a short arc.

"Hit 'em with the lead and the grapnel—"

Sara was backing out from under the foredeck. She laid *Loon's* wooden boat hook on the starboard bench. The boat hook's business end was shod with a heavy bronze hook ending in a massive, blunt point.

"—and the boat hook," Jon continued. "But we've got to get close enough to reach them. And they have a gun."

Jon looked to astern. "Looks like they're going to come alongside to windward."

Come alongside to windward . . .

"Ab. If they come by to windward, take a run at 'em and lay *Loon* right alongside. So we can hit 'em with these things."

"Okay," Abbie said instantly, without a quaver. She reached for the mainsheet.

Jon had been standing on the port bench abaft Abbie. Now he stepped up onto *Loon's* transom, his body swaying to her motion, and his left foot against the after through-bolted mainsheet block. His new perch would give him some extra height when he threw the grapnel over the sea skiff's engine—but he had nothing to hold onto.

Miguel was down in the cockpit, just forward of Abbie but abaft *Loon*'s port shroud. Sara crouched on the floorboards forward of Miguel, the business end of the boat hook propped on the forward coaming. Sara kept her right hand on the middle of the shaft.

"Here they come!"

A white blur snarled across their stern. The sea skiff's powerful engine sank to a low grumble as she slowed to match the little sloop's speed. A high-pitched squeal carried clearly over the grumbling engine and the splash and hiss of the two boats' wakes. "You punk kids! Come into the wind and get them sails down! Now!"

Must be Orcutt, Sara thought. *Funny. This was the first time they'd heard his voice.*

Jon looked down at the hood bent over the helm. "Not yet, Abbie. Steady as you go. Keep looking out of the corner of your eye. When you can see 'em, put the helm down and lay us right alongside. Don't worry how hard you hit 'em, just don't ram 'em head on. We want to wind up alongside." Jon turned. "Meeg, go for the big guy at the wheel. Right away. Really let him have it! Hard as you can!"

Miguel swung his lead in a short arc, testing its heft. He looked across at the water. The sea skiff was a high-sided boat, higher than their cockpit. He'd stand on the bench, Miguel decided, and swing the lead around his head. Really get that sucker humming, the way he had in mid-August. (His soccer ball confiscated yet again, a bored Miguel had borrowed *Loon*'s lead and line to "practice" his sounding skills. This time Miguel had destroyed a large terra cotta planter containing hot pink petunias, variegated cotoneasters, and a ceramic statuette of the infant Samuel at prayer.)

Miguel thought of the stone-dead eyes that had so terrified him. *I'll go for Orcutt, all right. You better believe I'll let him have it. Right in the snot locker, Orcutt baby, right in the snot locker.*

"Sara, wait 'til Miguel fires his lead. Meeg, after you fire that lead, drop down flat to give Sara a clear shot. Sara, harpoon whichever one of 'em's closest. Hard as you can." Sara's pale hood nodded. "I'm going to throw the grapnel over the engine and foul their prop. Everybody set?"

Orcutt's high voice had been squeaking at them while Jon organized the attack. Now the shrill voice raged, "You punk rats, you get them sails off *now!*"

Abbie sneaked a quick look over her left shoulder. "Jon! I can see their bow!"

"Wait for it, Abbie. They have to be almost parallel."

The breeze lightened. *Loon* straightened and slowed. The sea skiff surged ahead.

"Stand by!" Abbie hissed. The three others braced themselves.

"Do what Orcutt says!" Turco yelled. "Get them sails off *now* or I *SHOOT!*"

Then Abbie saw what she had been looking for out of the corner of her eye. The sea skiff was a boat-length away, her bow moving slowly abreast *Loon*'s steering station.

Abbie pushed the tiller to starboard, slowly at first and then faster. As the wind came farther forward, Abbie straddled the tiller and steered with her knees so that she could trim the mainsail with both hands. *Loon* heeled over and charged straight at the sea skiff's bow. The instant *Loon* turned toward the wind, her spinnaker flogged noisily in the brisk breeze with sharp *claps* that sounded like pistol shots.

~~~

After he shouted, "*SHOOT!*" Turco turned to Orcutt. He had been going to ask Orcutt if it was too late to make the kids sail up to *Thresher*. But Turco stopped. Something had just occurred to him that might solve all their problems. Maybe, he thought, they should turn to the alternative Craven had suggested that afternoon.

Then something else occurred to Turco. He looked into the darkness to windward. "Where the — is she?" he asked his enormous mate. "Do you hear her?"

Turco and Orcutt were peering into the darkness to port, searching for *Thresher*, when *Loon* began her attack run and her spinnaker started flogging.

Both men jerked violently around. For a split second Turco's brain rejected what his eyes were telling it. The little sloop was rushing directly at him with a bone of white water in her teeth. That little sail was flogging violently—*clap! Clap-clap!* She was only feet away! She was going to ram them!

Turco forgot that he was armed with an automatic pistol. He forgot that he could do whatever he wanted to these helpless kids and their dinky sailboat. In his sudden panic, desperate to escape the juggernaut rushing at him, Turco backed against Orcutt. Finding his way blocked, Turco dropped his pistol, turned, and tried to shove past Orcutt's huge bulk to the far side of the sea skiff. Orcutt wouldn't budge. Turco began screaming, a long, protracted *"YIIIIIIEEEE!"* while he clawed at Orcutt with both hands.

By that time *Loon* was barely twenty feet from the side of the sea skiff and charging directly at the two thieves. A burst of power might have shot the sea skiff clear of the little sailboat's charge, but the clawing, screaming Turco blocked Orcutt from the throttle. And then it was too late.

Just before *Loon* plunged headlong into the sea skiff, Abbie hauled the tiller hard to windward and let the mainsheet run. *Loon* fell off the wind and slammed her port side into the sea skiff just abeam the console with a loud *bang!*

Both boats shook. *Loon*'s boom bounced high into the air and snapped down. In the cockpit Miguel staggered but kept his feet. With nothing to hold onto, Jon teetered wildly on the transom. Abbie reached up and seized his jacket just before he toppled into the sea skiff. Then she trimmed the mainsheet hard and held the tiller over to starboard to keep *Loon* jammed against the bigger boat's side. If Orcutt turned the sea skiff to port, he would simply push her harder against *Loon*'s side.

"NOW, Miguel!"

Standing on the port bench, his shins braced against *Loon*'s coaming, the enraged Miguel swept the lead around his head with both hands. Once, twice, three times—the humming lead gathered speed with each sweep.

As the lead hummed around Miguel's head, and Abbie bent double to avoid being brained, the screaming, clawing Turco had managed to shove Orcutt to the port edge of the backless steering bench. Just before he fell off the bench, Orcutt grabbed the edge of the steering console with his left hand, wrenched his right arm free of Turco's clutching hands, and with a lethal sweep, sent the little man flying backward over the steering bench and into the after well. Orcutt then stood, turned toward *Loon*, and felt for the sea skiff's throttle. As Miguel released his lead, Orcutt was facing directly at him.

The humming lead shot across the gunwales of the two boats and caught Orcutt, not in the "snot locker," as Miguel had hoped, but in the center of his chest with a *whump* that was clearly audible above the snarl of the sea skiff's engine. The enormous figure toppled backward across the steering bench and fell into the after well on top of Turco.

"Take *that*, you——!" Miguel screamed, dancing with excitement. Then he threw the coils of the sounding line across the sea skiff and dropped to a crouch on the floorboards.

Jon heard the hollow *whump* and saw Orcutt collapse on top of the struggling Turco. Then he concentrated on his part in the attack.

The huge white engine was clearly visible in the starlight. Jon swung his grapnel forward, backward, then tossed it up and over the sea skiff's transom. He heard the grapnel bounce once on the engine's shroud and saw it briefly as it vanished on the far side of the engine. The line led forward of the engine. Jon paid out what he hoped was enough slack, then tugged on the grapnel's rode to pull it up and into the propeller. He yanked again. The line was stuck on something. Jon yanked harder, once, twice, a third enormous yank. The outboard grumbled on, its note unchanged.

Jon's heart sank. The grapnel wasn't hitting the propeller. The captainless sea skiff was slowly grinding its way along *Loon*'s side. Sick that he had failed the others, Jon threw the rest of the line into the water on the near side of the sea skiff and stepped down onto the port bench. *Maybe the slack will foul the prop. . . .*

Jon was about to turn away from the sea skiff when he saw something move in her after well. It was Turco. He had regained his feet. His outstretched right hand held something that glistened dully in the faint light.

Crouched on the cockpit floorboards, Sara and Miguel saw Jon raise his arms in front of his face. Miguel shot to his feet. Turco was pointing something at Jon and screaming unintelligibly.

Without thinking, Miguel jumped from the port bench onto *Loon*'s broad starboard deck. Balancing easily in the slight swell, Miguel noticed that he now towered over Turco.

Miguel heard a *click* as metal slid against metal. Without a moment's hesitation, he took two dancing steps down the deck and aimed a sweeping, sideways kick at the pistol in Turco's hands. Miguel heard a sharp *crack!*, saw a brief flash, and felt something bite into his foot as his sweeping kick drove Turco's pistol into his face, snapping the little man's head back and driving him forward across the steering bench.

The force of Miguel's sideways kick spun him around so that he was facing forward. He did not see Turco fall between the bench and the console. Miguel was suddenly fighting for balance. His left foot was so numb he couldn't feel the deck under it.

Throughout Jon's and Miguel's furious assault, the sea skiff had been grinding its way along *Loon*'s port side. The teetering Miguel, now balancing on his right foot and desperate not to fall into the sea skiff's cockpit, had been carried abeam *Loon*'s mast. If he didn't move quickly, he would be carried clear past the sloop's bow with no way of getting back aboard. Pushing off with his right foot, Miguel leaped for *Loon*'s foredeck.

He landed on both feet. He was reaching for the spinnaker pole to keep himself upright when his feet slipped out from under him and he sat down hard. As he slid across the slippery foredeck, he managed to hook the spinnaker foreguy with his left arm, just saving himself from shooting under the jib and into the black water. He scrambled aft on all fours and dove head first over the coaming into the cockpit.

From her crouched position on the floorboards, Sara had seen Turco raise his arm and point something at Jon, which she knew very well was that black pistol; she saw Miguel step up onto the sea skiff's gunwale, take his two dancing steps aft, and launch his tremendous kick at Turco; she heard a sharp crack; she saw Miguel leap onto *Loon*'s foredeck, check his slide with the foreguy, and fall into the cockpit.

He's all right, Sara thought. *He's all right.*

Then pent-up rage swept away Sara's fear and relief.

Sara lifted the boathook, stepped up onto *Loon's* port bench, and looked down into the sea skiff. Orcutt, who was trying to pull himself to his feet using the backless steering seat for support, was right below her.

Sara raised her heavy weapon with both hands, drew it back, aimed it at Orcutt's head with her left hand, and threw as hard as she could with her right. As the boat hook left her hands, Sara screamed, *"YAAAAAAAAH!"*

Pain saved Orcutt from a certain, almost Homeric death. Every time he moved, dreadful stabs across his chest made him catch his breath. One of these terrible arrows of pain pierced him just as Sara threw. Orcutt gasped and bent over the steering bench. The boat hook whistled through the space where his head had just been.

As Orcutt collapsed onto the steering bench, Turco's head rose slowly, forward of the steering bench but just below the untended steering wheel, and just below the arc of the boat hook that Sara had aimed at Orcutt.

Little Turco's long day had been a series of inexplicable calamities. By some miracle the brother and sister had managed to find and lift the second sack off the bottom of the Graveyard. If the sea skiff hadn't reached the Graveyard early, the punk kids would've gotten clean away. Then, once the little rats were safely locked in the *Thresher's* cabin and the situation completely under control, two *other* punk kids had appeared from nowhere and freed them. And now, just when he and Orcutt had tracked all four of them down and the situation was *again* under control, the little sloop had attacked—when their *backs* were turned, the little rats!—and rammed the sea skiff. And then when he tried to shoot one of the little rats, some tremendous *thing* had knocked his gun into his face. His jaw must be broken. Where was that pistol . . . ?

Clawing at the deck under the steering bench, the dazed little man tried, for the second time, to find his weapon, but the pistol seemed to have vanished. He was pulling himself up by the bench when the boat hook hissed by his head. Turco screamed shrilly and sank out of sight.

If Sara's javelin missed Orcutt and Turco, it did *not* miss the steering console. The heavy bronze fitting on the oak boat hook passed between two spokes of the steering wheel, crashed clean through the console's rotten plywood, and thudded into the sea skiff's port-side planking. As long as the boat hook remained fixed there, Orcutt and Turco would be unable to steer their boat.

The sea skiff bumped once more against *Loon*'s side. Then it scraped free and curved away to port. Its low-pitched snarl fell astern. Once again *Loon*'s crew could hear the steady hiss of the quarter wake, the sigh of the wind, and the rhythmic creaking of the wooden spars as *Loon* plugged along for home.

Jon sank onto the port bench. His hands were trembling. He looked across the cockpit. Sara was sitting forward of Abbie on the starboard bench. Miguel was slumped on the floorboards, his head between his knees.

"Godfrey. Is everybody okay?"

Sara stretched her sea boot across the cockpit and nudged his foot. "I'm okay. What about you?"

"I think I'm okay. He must have missed me. And I missed their engine." Jon looked at Abbie. "You all right, Ab?"

"Me? All I did was sit here."

Sara snorted. "All!"

Jon looked at the dark shape huddled on the floorboards. "You okay, Meeg?"

No answer.

"Must be asleep," Sara said. "I don't blame him. Wait'll you hear what he did."

"Yeah, what happened back there?" Jon clenched his hands to stop them trembling.

"It was Miguel. Kicked the gun right into the little guy's face just as he shot. Then Meeg jumped onto the foredeck and did a somersault into the cockpit."

They looked at the dark figure huddled on the floorboards. "Meeg," Jon whispered. "You saved my life."

The huddled figure sagged back against the starboard bench. "Sara. My foot's all numb," said a faint voice. "I think I'm gonna be sick."

"*Miguel!*" Sara dropped to her knees. The searchlight clicked on. "Jon! There's blood *every*where."

~~~

After Jon cut away Miguel's boot with his rigging knife, Sara wrapped the foot in a soggy towel while Jon swished his hands over the starboard side. Then he sat next to Abbie and looked over the bow.

The lights of Old Town stretched in a sparkling band down their starboard side, closer now than when the battle with the sea skiff had begun. Jon estimated the bearing of the green flasher, then looked under the boom at West Head light. He hoped they were far enough north to clear the Brick Pile.

"Really close now, Jonno."

Before Jon could answer, the sea skiff's engine, which had been rumbling sullenly on their port quarter, soared to an angry, full-speed snarl.

"Haven't they had enough?" Abbie asked grimly.

Jon groped behind the starboard bench. "We've got the spare tiller."

"Pump handle," came a groggy voice from the floorboards. "Gimme pump handle. . . ."

The sea skiff's engine began to howl.

"Those—." Jon hefted the spare tiller, a beautifully balanced curve of oak with a thick butt. Jon looked forward. "Sara, slide Miguel under. . . ."

Suddenly, as if a knife had cut a throat, the sea skiff's engine stopped.

In the sudden quiet, *Loon*'s crew could hear again the pleasant, dry creaking of her wooden spars and the hiss of her stern wake. Abbie bowed her head on the tiller. "Oh God," she sobbed. "Oh, thank you, God."

"You *didn't* miss!" Sara whispered. She stretched her free hand toward Jon.

Jon was too tired to speak. He squeezed the cold hand holding his. "Almost home," he whispered back.

Schoodic Head Finds *Loon*

9:15 p.m., Labor Day, September 4

Commander Selph stood quietly at the back of *Schoodic Head*'s bridge. His orders had gotten the search organized. His job now was to let *Schoodic*'s skipper and crew search for the four children.

As *Schoodic Head* roared past R "2," her blue Grimes light flashing, one of the watch standers on the bridge reported a light on the port beam.

The *Schoodic*'s skipper, a twenty-six-year-old lieutenant (junior grade), trained his glasses to port. "Got it."

Commander Selph leaned forward.

"It's an S-O-S, Captain."

The deck vibrated as the eighty-three-footer's powerful engines increased their revolutions. The *Schoodic Head* heeled to port, then came to an even keel as she steadied on her new course and charged through the night, rolling slightly in the beam seas. The only sound was the relentless roar of her powerful engines.

A few minutes later, the *Schoodic*'s skipper lowered his binoculars. "Sir, I've got two vessels in sight. Starboard ten I've got a white-hulled powerboat. Looks to be dead in the water. No sign of crew. Broad on the port bow I've got a little white sailboat—white sails, looks like." Commander Selph caught a flash of teeth. "Sir, I think that must be *Loon*."

In five minutes *Schoodic* was approaching the little sloop. Out on the port wing of the bridge, Commander Selph raised his borrowed glasses. White hull. White sails. The perky little loon on the mainsail.

Three pale faces peered up at them from the cockpit. *Sara . . . Jon . . . Abbie . . . Where's Miguel?*

Schoodic turned to port until she was paralleling *Loon's* course, then slowed and coasted alongside to windward of the little sloop. *Loon's* sails sagged and she sat upright.

Looking down at the three pale faces below him, Commander Selph stifled the impulse to roar, "Where the *devil* have you been?" Instead he called, "We've been worried about you. Where's Miguel?"

Sara ducked out of sight, then struggled back into view. Her arm was around Miguel. His dark head was resting against her shoulder.

"My God," Commander Selph whispered.

"Dad!" Sara yelled. "Me and Miguel found the second bag—"

Commander Selph's jaw dropped.

"—but Craven's gang got there early and captured us."

Commander Selph turned speechlessly to the young skipper. Then he turned back to *Loon*.

"They made us take *Phoenix* to Porpoise Island. Craven had us locked up on the *Thresher*. Jon and Abbie came after us in *Loon* and found us."

"We got clean away," Jon yelled. "Then the sea skiff caught us back there."

Abbie shot to her feet. "Commander!" she shrieked. "We attacked the sea skiff! We creamed 'em!"

"Attacked the sea skiff?" Commander Selph repeated softly, half to himself. "Attacked the sea skiff?"

Before he could answer, Abbie shrieked, "It's back there somewhere!" She gestured violently at the murk astern. "There's two hurt men in it. They may be dead," she added hopefully.

Miguel's dark head lifted from Sara's shoulder. "Dad!" came a faint voice. His father could barely hear him. "I kicked Turco's gun out of his hand but I got a little shot!" The dark head sank back.

A little shot?

"Sara," roared her frantic father, "how badly is Miguel *hurt?*"

Schoodic Head was drawing ahead of *Loon*. The eighty-three-footer's big engines rumbled briefly, and then the two vessels, the towering eighty-three-footer and the little white sloop, were again in company.

"Dad, it's not *too* bad," Sara called. She was directly below him again, sitting on the floorboards, her back against the starboard bench, Miguel's head against her shoulder. "I think they shot off some of Miguel's toes. Two of them, maybe. It's kind of hard to tell."

"Jee-*zus!*"

"Meeg was bleeding a lot at first, but we got the bleeding slowed down, right, Meeg?"

Miguel waved feebly.

"Miguel feels kind of sick and cold and tired, but I think we can get in okay. We're pretty close now."

Loon was beginning to move out from the lee cast by *Schoodic*'s high sides. Her spinnaker filled with a sudden *flap!* and she heeled. Again the powerful engines rumbled and the eighty-three-footer slid up beside the little sloop. *Loon*'s sails swung inboard.

Commander Selph looked over *Schoodic*'s bow. R "2" was a quarter of a mile away.

"Sara," he called down, "if you're sure the bleeding's under control, it would save time if you took him right in. We'll call for a thirty-six-footer to meet you, and there'll be an ambulance waiting at the station."

Schoodic's skipper nodded and reached for the radio's microphone.

"We can make it!" Jon called. "Commander! The second bag's on the *Thresher*! The *Thresher* was northeast of us when we attacked the sea skiff. Her lights are out."

Miguel's voice was weak but clear. "Dad! I'll be okay. Go get the *Thresher*!" His head sagged back against Sara's shoulder.

Commander Selph cleared his throat. He hoped the young skipper couldn't hear the wobble in his voice. "Don't worry, Miguel. We'll get 'em!"

Schoodic Head had drawn ahead of *Loon*. The little sloop's sails filled again, and she heeled. "You'll be home soon. Well done!" He raised his arm high overhead.

Thin cheers followed the *Schoodic* as she drew away.

Commander Selph stayed on the bridge wing for a few moments, looking astern. *Loon*'s crew was dousing her spinnaker as she rounded R "2" for the last leg into Old Town.

Sailors Home

12:05 a.m., Tuesday, September 5–
Thursday, September 7

As *Loon* jibed onto the starboard tack and started to run slowly toward R "4 and the shelter of West Head, a thirty-six-footer roared toward them, a white bone in her teeth. The thirty-six-footer throttled back, circled astern of *Loon*, and eased alongside to leeward.

"Hey, Jon!"

"Smitty!"

Smitty was a second-class quartermaster from Oklahoma and a good friend of the twins and Sara.

"Can you make it into the float?"

"You bet!"

Smitty waved. The thirty-six-footer moved farther off their port side and kept station as the little white sloop sailed slowly past R "4," rolling slightly in the leftover chop washing around West Head. Ten minutes later, when they turned to starboard at R "6", the twins and Sara could see a flashing red light at the Coast Guard Station. *The ambulance waiting for Miguel,* Sara thought.

Jon dropped the jib on deck as Abbie turned *Loon* into the wind and coasted alongside the float reserved for the station's small boats. As *Loon* slid gently up to the float, four waiting Coast Guardsmen made her fast as Jon lowered the mainsail. Then a kind of controlled frenzy broke out.

Cops carrying a stretcher ran down the brow to the float. Two of the four Coasties boarded *Loon*, inspected Miguel briefly—his left foot was still swathed in the blood-soaked towel—then picked him up and handed him to the two sailors on the float. They in turn deposited Miguel on the stretcher. The cops carried him gently up the brow to his mother. The three friends, still aboard *Loon*, saw her bend over the stretcher as Miguel reached out his hand. Then he was lifted into the waiting ambulance. Marie Selph climbed in after him, followed by a nurse. The ambulance siren began to wail as the vehicle turned and sped out of the station, bound for the Great Whale Island cottage hospital.

Betty Cooper, Chief Cooper, Sergeant Maciel, and two state troopers were standing on the float looking down into Loon's cockpit. The three friends braced themselves. But Betty Cooper only smiled and said, "Are we glad to see you. We have been so worried."

Chief Cooper nodded.

"You must be exhausted," Betty Cooper said. "Let's go home. You come too, Sara. Your mom's going to stay with Miguel until she's sure he's okay."

Abbie fell into her mother's arms and began to sob. Sara, too worried and scared to cry, tottered after them up the brow to hard land. Jon was almost asleep on his feet, but he stayed on the float, first to check *Loon*'s cracked port sheer strake, then to help the Coasties stow *Loon*'s mainsail, rig fenders, and secure her to the float with proper spring lines. Only then did Jon follow the others.

Early Tuesday Morning

Safe at last in the Coopers' house, the three friends showered away the dried salt and the Porpoise Island sand and put on clean (and warm!) pajamas. Sara had to borrow a pair of Abbie's, which were a little on the short side.

Betty Cooper cleaned Sara's cuts (*Ow!*), painted them with iodine (*ow-ow-ow-ow-OW!*), and bandaged her hands. She inspected the twins for injuries (*Mom!*). Then the tired adventurers were fed and put to bed.

They slept pretty well, considering. They never heard Betty Cooper peek in during the night: at Jon in his bunkroom, and at Abbie and Sara tucked up in the twin beds in Abbie's room.

Early Tuesday Afternoon

Ellie Madeiros whistled. "Barnacles did all that?"

"Yep," Sara said offhandedly.

The emergency room nurse shook her head as she chucked Betty Cooper's home-made bandages into the waste bin. She had seen more barnacle cuts than she could remember, but these were some wicked cuts. *Most people get away from barnacles after their first slice,* she thought. *What was this girl thinking of? Her hands are like hamburger!*

Sara and the twins were questioned separately later Tuesday afternoon by state police officers from Gardiners Port. When the three talked later, they realized they had each been led, step by step, and by remarkably similar questions, through every moment of their adventures, with many follow-up questions about particular details.

One older officer was clearly skeptical about their stories, especially Sara's account of how Miguel solved the mystery of the de Parque burglary. "You say he figured all that out from a *dream?*"

"That's how it all started," Sara replied.

"They're questioning the suspects now over in Gardiners Port," the skeptic told her. "We'll see if they say anything about that little trolling engine.

"Now," he continued unpleasantly. "This so-called message." He flicked the brown scrap lying on the table before him. "*How* did you figure out what it meant?"

The state troopers spent little time asking the twins and Sara about *Phoenix's* foray up the Lane to retrieve the second bag of treasure, or about *Loon's* patrolling out in Whale Sound. Most astonishing of all, the troopers weren't especially interested when the twins and Sara tried to tell them, separately, how Orcutt and Turco had gotten so badly injured or how Sara had jammed the sea skiff's steering or how Jon had disabled the huge outboard.

None of these heroics seemed to matter. The state police were mostly interested in the sea skiff's pursuit and gunpoint capture of *Phoenix* and in the Selph kids' incarceration aboard *Thresher*. The troopers did make sure, over and over, that all four friends had heard Turco threaten to shoot, that three of them had seen Turco point his pistol at Jon, that all four had heard the gunshot and seen the muzzle flash just as Miguel kicked the gun into his face. Not before, not after, but *as*.

The three friends also noticed, with mixed feelings, that while the troopers asked repeatedly—*When* did you do this? *What* did you see? *Where* did that happen? *Who* did that? *How* did you know that?—not once did they ask the three friends, *Why* did you do what you did?

Tuesday night Sara realized that her father knew most of the story. He didn't ask her a single question, however. He said only, "We'll all talk about it after Miguel comes home."

Chief Cooper also knew most of the saga. He told his twins what Commander Selph had told Sara: the two families would meet at the Selphs' when Miguel was home.

Wednesday

The twins and Sara started school Wednesday morning just as if nothing had happened over the weekend. Before the three friends met to walk to the old Grange School, both sets of parents had told them to say as little as possible about what they'd been up to over the holiday weekend.

"Just say you were runnin' around in your boats and *Phoenix* ran out of gas," Chief Cooper had advised the twins. The Selphs said the same to Sara.

During the ninth- and tenth-graders' noisy reunion in front of the school steps before Miss Dillon rang the warning bell, everyone wanted to know about Sara's bandaged hands.

"Barnacles," she said again, and they, too, nodded.

"You climbin' on rocks?" Wobbly Vincent, a ninth-grader, jigged impatiently from foot to foot, his head rocking from side to side, as he waited for Sara's answer.

Sara shook her head. "Anchor line, Wob."

"Oh. Yeah. Anchor line," Wob said. He nodded knowingly, still jigging from foot to foot. Then he jigged away up the steps and vanished into the dark interior of the Old Grange.

And that's the truth, Sara thought. *As far as it goes.*

During recess, the fifth-graders mobbed Sara. "Miguel's in the hospital? What happened?"

"His foot got hurt. Real bad," Sara said. "He was practicing his kicking." And that seemed to satisfy the fifth-graders.

That's true, too, Sara thought. *But it's not the whole story.*

Since Sara couldn't hold a pencil or turn pages, Jon wrote down her assignments and took notes as she sat next to him. He carried her books home at the end of the school day. When they reached the Selphs' house, Jon put the books on the Selphs' kitchen table and said good night. During the school week there was no visiting between the four friends' houses.

As of Wednesday night, although nothing official had been said, everyone on Great Whale Island knew *something* had happened. Old Mrs. Atherton out at Eastville near the Opening was especially sure something had happened. What it was *exactly*, Mrs. Atherton could not say, but she had a shrewd suspicion that Communists were at the root of it.

"You mark my words," she said ominously, shaking her finger at her skeptical Eastville neighbors. "It's *them*."

Some folks knew that *Loon* and *Phoenix* had left Old Town in thick weather on Labor Day. Other folks knew that neither boat had returned to Shellfish Bay by evening. A lot of folks knew about the flurry of Coast Guard activity Monday, especially *Schoodic* departing that night with the group commander aboard. Many folks knew that the Cooper and Selph kids had returned to Old Town late Monday evening aboard *Loon* and docked at the Coast Guard Station. Many Old Towners were wondering what had happened to the little green dory.

About one strand in the story there was no mystery, however. *Everyone* knew that Miguel Selph had been lifted out of *Loon* and taken by ambulance to the cottage hospital with a broken leg that might have to be amputated—or maybe it was appendicitis.

Thursday

The *Thresher* gang was arraigned Thursday morning in Gardiners Port. Every local newspaper and radio reporter was in Superior Court that morning. According to the stories broadcast at noon on local and network radio stations, the state had charged the four thieves with attempted murder (Turco had aimed and fired his pistol at an unnamed "child"), assault with a deadly weapon (Turco had shot another unnamed child in the foot), kidnapping (the thieves had seized two children and imprisoned them aboard *Thresher*), and, most unusually for mid-twentieth-century New England, piracy (the gang had seized one of the two boats sailed by the minor children and had attempted to seize the other).

Though the four "children" were not named in court, they were identified as residents of Great Whale Island and their boats were described as well. That was enough for the local reporters.

They started pouring into Old Town Thursday afternoon, some by ferry, some by chartered boat. One enterprising and well-funded columnist chartered a seaplane. More followed on Friday. All of them wanted desperately to be the first to interview and photograph the amazing kids who had solved the de Parque burglary and then gone after the thieves themselves.

Chief Cooper was ready for them. So was the rest of Great Whale Island. Wherever reporters, photographers, and radio "personalities" went seeking their quarry, they were sent off on wild goose chases or referred to the police station.

By all accounts, Flutie Cuzzone, one of Sara's and the twins' classmates, came up with the best wild goose chase of them all. When she was cornered by a reporter-photographer team outside the old Grange School Friday morning before school, Flutie said she thought she knew where the three were.

"I heard they're hiding from you reporters," the inspired Flutie told the team. "With old Mrs. Atherton."

Flutie gave the reporters directions to Eastville, the cluster of weathered cottages huddled behind the dunes out near the Opening.

"Look for the cottage flying a really big American flag," Flutie told the reporters. "You can't miss it."

The two newshounds roared off in a rented jalopy, trailed closely by three other rented jalopies and Old Town's only "taxi," all Model As jam-packed with predatory reporters who smelled a scoop. The four old cars *ow-OOO-ga*'ed the whole way out to Eastville, leaving behind them a thick trail of dust and sulfurous language as they tried to pass each other on the rutted shore road.

The conspiratorial-minded Mrs. Atherton was snatched from her radio by the squealing of car brakes, followed by a furious banging on her door and confused shouts of, "Where are they? Let us in! Send them out! We want to do a photo shoot! Photo shoot!"

Mrs. Atherton gasped, then **grabbed** the earpiece from her wall telephone and frantically jiggled the hook. "Laura! It's me! Them communists got me surrounded! Tell the Chief! They're a-goin' to shoot!"

Then Mrs. Atherton seized her late husband's clam rake from its wall hook and prepared for battle.

~~~

Reporters who went to the station were politely received and given a remarkably vague briefing on Monday's events. According to the *Clarion*'s reporter, Chief Cooper told one disappointed group,

> The district attorney has specifically directed that the details of these events be kept confidential until the trial. . . . No, the children are not available for photographs or interviews. One of them is still hospitalized. The other three are trying to return to normal life. They started school yesterday. Only minor injuries to the older three kids. Thank you for your understanding.

When the dejected reporters left for their chartered boats or the ferry, they had no exclusive photos and no interviews to write up. All they had to show for their efforts was a mimeographed sheet bearing the official explanation of the apprehension of the *Thresher* gang.

And that, so far as Great Whale Islanders knew, was the end of the story.

~~~

Commander Selph didn't get a chance to write his official report until Thursday afternoon. After proofreading its lifeless, formal language, he sat back in his office chair and relived what had really happened that moonless night.

It had taken a good three hours for *Schoodic*, roaring through moderate seas at flank speed, to close within three thousand yards of the fleeing black boat.

First over the short-wave radio, then over both the radio and her powerful loud hailer, *Schoodic* ordered the fugitive to "heave to or we will open fire!"

Thresher ran unchecked for the open Atlantic, her stern wake foaming out behind her.

After *Thresher* had ignored the fourth order to heave to, *Schoodic* fired a warning shot well ahead of *Thresher* so that its splash would be clearly visible from the fleeing vessel's wheelhouse. *Thresher*'s speed did not slacken.

Again *Schoodic*'s deck gun barked. Again the splash, clearly visible from *Schoodic*'s bridge. *Thresher* ran on.

"Fire for effect," Commander Selph ordered.

The third round from *Schoodic*'s deck gun was slightly short. The gun crew elevated the 20-millimeter's barrel and fired.

Everyone on *Schoodic*'s bridge saw the red glow of a direct hit, then what appeared to be a secondary explosion in *Thresher*'s wheelhouse. The black boat slewed violently to port and lost way.

When Commander Selph and three sailors, all carrying drawn .45 automatics, peered into *Thresher*'s wheelhouse, they saw a grotesquely fat man lying face down on the deck and covered with shattered glass and splintered wood. A ten-foot section of steel lay across his back. His shirt was smoldering.

The fat man must have been steering *Thresher* when the fourth round from *Schoodic*'s deck gun blew the top of her mast clean off. The ten-foot section of red-hot steel had plunged through the wheelhouse roof, blowing glass shards and wood splinters throughout the structure. The hot steel must have hit the fat man full in the back like a blow from the flat of a sword, throwing him hard him against *Thresher*'s wheel, knocking him unconscious and setting fire to his shirt.

Once the smoldering shirt had been doused and the blubbery form manhandled onto the afterdeck, the three sailors went hunting for the second man they knew was aboard.

When a very large first-class boatswain's mate opened the watertight door to the chain locker, a tall man wearing a leather vest and clutching a yellow bundle tried to lunge through the narrow opening. The surprised boatswain jammed him hard against the edge of the doorway. The man dropped gasping to the deck as another petty officer hurried up the passageway, his .45 pointed upward.

The boatswain stooped, seized the yellow bundle Craven had been hugging, and hefted it.

"So, you." The boatswain prodded Craven with his size-thirteen boondocker. "This here what we're looking for?"

The only response was whooping gasps.

Holding the heavy parcel under one arm, the boatswain bent and jerked Craven to his feet. He spun Craven around, removed the long filleting knife from its sheath, and booted the prisoner, doubled over and gasping, along the passageway and up the companionway. Craven fell through the splintered door next to the base of the mast and collapsed on the after deck beside the semiconscious, groaning fat man.

A sailor secured Craven's hands behind him, then stood to one side. The first-class boatswain's mate stood on Craven's other side, his hand on his sidearm. The third sailor, his sidearm drawn, stood directly in front of Craven and Packy. Commander Selph then stepped forward.

Leaning forward in his office chair, Commander Selph flipped to the last page of his report. "The suspects were cautioned by the undersigned," he read. He stared at the emotionless sentence for a moment, then sat back and remembered what he had really said.

Staring down at the shackled figure sitting with bowed head, Commander Selph snapped, "You!"

No response.

"Look at me, you."

Slowly the bent head lifted until the two men, one sitting on the deck, the other looming over him, were looking into each other's eyes.

"My name is Selph. I am Commanding Officer of the Great Whale Island Coast Guard Group. You two are under arrest. Complete charges will be specified when you're arraigned in Gardners Port. As far as the United States Coast Guard is concerned, the charges are piracy, kidnapping, and attempted murder. You and the two in the other boat have unlawfully seized a vessel and kidnapped her crew, both children. You have attempted to seize another vessel and kidnap *her* crew, all of whom were children. The youngest of them is eleven. According to the children, the men in the other boat attempted to murder one if not all of the children. They succeeded only in wounding one of the children. The eleven-year-old."

Craven lowered his eyes.

"Look at me, you!" Commander Selph snapped.

Craven looked up.

"I gather that you are the leader of this gang that kidnaps and shoots children."

Craven looked away.

"In addition to being a Coast Guard officer, I am the father of the two children you kidnapped. You'll probably be wondering what happened to your sea skiff. The four children managed to disable it and are now safe in Old Town. The people aboard the sea skiff are both in custody. They are also both injured. The children's testimony against you is ensured. I'll leave you to imagine its effect on your future."

Craven remained silent. Commander Selph stared a moment at the lowered head. Only then did he issue his caution.

"Any statements you make may be used as evidence against you. Obey all orders instantly. If you resist, we will shoot you. "

Then he turned to the three sailors.

"Get 'em aboard!"

The Reckoning

After Dinner, Friday, September 8

Awood fire, the first of the season, crackled cheerfully in the Selphs' wood stove.

Miguel lay on the old sofa, his enormous white foot elevated on two pillows, an ice bag on top of the foot, and another pillow behind his head.

Sara had put a glass of chocolate milk on a low, tile-topped table where Miguel could reach it. She was sitting on a cane chair next to the table—in case Miguel needed anything. Jon was sitting next to her, Abbie next to Jon. Chief Cooper, standing beside the Packish Fuel Company calendar, was just finishing the official chronology of the de Parque robbery.

"That's the size of it," Chief Cooper said. "As far as we know it now. Robbery early last Thursday." He tapped the calendar. "Arraignment yesterday, just a week later. But Godfrey! What a week."

Staring at the calendar, Sara was suddenly overwhelmed by images from the past week: the first forbidden trip into the Graveyard—the voyage to Quarantine Island—deciphering the "POT" message—dragging the heavy yellow bundle aboard *Phoenix*—the sea skiff appearing suddenly behind them at the entrance to the Graveyard—the tattered quilt and mildewed pillow aboard *Thresher*—Miguel breathing quietly in the other bunk while she cried out silently for Mom and Dad.

It's all because of me we're here, she remembered crying into the sour-smelling pillow. *If Miguel gets hurt, it will be all my fault.*

The images kept flooding in. Sara saw Miguel jump onto the sea skiff's gunwale—saw the flash of the gunshot that shattered the night—saw the blood welling from Miguel's shredded boot when she clicked on the searchlight—saw *Schoodic*'s white bulk looming above *Loon*—felt again the mingled relief and overwhelming guilt when she saw her mother reach out to Miguel on his stretcher.

Sara's eyes began to prickle.

". . . so it was Turco by himself," Sara heard Chief Cooper say. The chief was smiling at Miguel from a wing chair opposite the sofa. Sara looked down through brimming eyes at her brother's dark, shaggy head.

"The others dropped Turco off in the sea skiff somewhere out in Butler's Bay. Then they went on to Gardners Port in *Thresher*. Turco went to Shellfish Bay through the Opening. Just as Miguel figured. My guess is Turco kept that cross back for himself and buried it so the others wouldn't know about it. They still don't know you found it, Miguel— and we're not going to tell them. Yet."

The chief's smile faded. He turned to his twins and Sara. When he spoke, he was again his dispassionate, impartial self.

"The Selphs agreed that we should get the police work out of the way and give Miguel time to get home before we had a two-family talk. Now it's time for that talk."

Alan Selph looked at the Sara and the twins. "We think the best thing would be for you to tell us the *whole* story. Right from the beginning."

Oh boy, thought Sara. She dabbed at her eyes with her bandaged hand, stifled a sob, and looked at Jon. "You first," she managed to say.

"I guess it all started," Jon began, his elbows on his knees and staring at the carpet, "when Sergeant Maciel told us about those outboard noises the night of the burglary. When Miguel heard about the outboard noises, he remembered his dream that night. . . ."

And Jon explained everything that had happened from the moment Miguel found the cross up to the four friends' float-planned trip to Sei Island. But when he reached the moment off the Graveyard when Sara said, "Just for fun . . . ," he faltered.

"I don't know quite how it happened." Jon fumbled. "But . . . ah . . . all at once we were . . . sort of . . ."

"It was me."

Everyone turned to Sara.

"What do you mean?" her father asked.

Sara stared down at her lap, took a deep breath, and plunged ahead. "I took *Phoenix* into the Graveyard to find out what the channel was like. To see if we could do it. Jon and Abbie didn't want to go in, but I was skipper. I decided."

Sara raised frightened eyes.

Her father's blue eyes bored into hers. "You took *Phoenix* into the Graveyard?"

"Yes."

Alan Selph's voice rose. "Where I told you *never* to go?" He was staring at Sara as if she were a stranger.

Marie Selph reached out a slender dark hand and placed it on his arm. For a moment the two parents looked at each other. Then Alan Selph turned back to Sara. "Go on."

Sara looked at Jon.

"It was pretty scary," Jon admitted. "The current kept shoving us all over the place. Then we got to these three weird rollers. . . ."

As the story of the first trip into the Graveyard unfolded, the four adults looked less and less like outraged parents and more and more like spellbound listeners.

At length Jon reached the moment when they had figured out the meaning of the strange E POT message.

"But Jon," Tom Cooper cried. "When you figured out what that message meant, why didn't you come to me?"

"Abbie and Miguel wanted to," Sara said softly. Miguel stared at his bandaged foot. "I told them Jon and I were going to find the second bag ourselves and nothing was going to stop us, and if they didn't want to go, they didn't have to. When I said that, they said they'd go."

Jon started to speak, but Sara flashed him a watery blue look.

"I said nothing would happen." Sara's voice quavered. "Miguel asked could we get there early." Another tear started down her cheek. "We didn't get there early enough. Meeg got shot." Sara looked at Jon. "And you almost got killed. I'd rather die than have anything happen to you. Or Miguel. Or Ab."

Jon was appalled to feel moisture welling up in his eyes. This was *not* supposed to happen anymore.

"That's not all of it, Dad," he croaked. He cleared his throat and looked squarely at his father. "I thought of going to you, too. But then . . ."

Jon bit off what he had been about to say. This was not the time to tell his father that he, Jon, was going to be taller.

". . . but then I thought, it's little kids that go to their parents. It's little kids that run away. And we're not little kids anymore. So I told the others we'd started something and been right all along and now we should finish what we'd started. On our own."

Jon looked at Miguel. "Looking for the second bag was too dangerous. I'm sorry, Meeg."

"*I'm* not sorry," Miguel said stoutly.

Sara left her chair, knelt, and laid her head on the cushions beside Miguel.

"Aw, Sara." Hesitantly, awkwardly, Miguel put a bandaged hand on Sara's head. "*Shoot!* The foot's okay. Only *little* parts got shot off." Miguel waved away the little parts with his other bandaged hand. "Just ends of the middle toes. I've still got most of my big toe and all of the little one. Doc Skillings says *they're* the ones I need to play soccer with."

Sara buried her face in her elbow. As she sobbed, she once again saw herself walking up time's endless path, leaving a trail of black footprints behind her.

Alan Selph rose quickly and went to the cane chair. "Here, Sara. Here."

Sara looked up at her father. He lifted her to her feet and laid her head against his shoulder, much as he had done when she was little.

Tom Cooper was frowning at his twins. "I admire what you said about standing on your own two feet. And you're dead right. I probably *wouldn't* have believed the story about an outboard in a dream. Or your interpretation of that Pot message." The chief's frown deepened. "But I want you to know that three fifteen-year-olds and an eleven-year-old have *no* business tangling with armed crooks. That is work for law enforcement authorities and for no one else.

"Finally," Chief Cooper said ominously. He looked from Jon to Abbie. "We are going to discuss this Graveyard business." Jon felt his stomach somersault. "When we get home. Those float plans never said one word about the Graveyard."

Sara looked up. As she wiped at her tears, she saw that her mother was wearing what her husband always called her Queen Look. When Marie Selph addressed Tom Cooper, she spoke with dignity and precision.

"I am a proud mother. I have brave children. And they have very brave friends. Your twins saved Sara and Miguel. You should be proud of them."

Tom Cooper banged the arm of his chair. "Dog*gone* it, Marie!" He looked almost embarrassed. "For Pete's sake! I *am* proud of them. Of *course* I'm proud of them." Tom Cooper's voice softened. "Sorry. I'm just trying not to let it show," he said sheepishly. "Until after our discussion."

Tom Cooper turned to the four friends. He seemed to slump a little in the wing chair. "You've all got real guts, but none of this should've ever happened. None of it. Godfrey! When I think of Jonno standing up there with that—" Here Tom Cooper used a regrettable word, but not as regrettable as the word Jon had used just before the Battle with the Sea Skiff— ". . . aiming a gun at him . . . Miguel, if you hadn't . . ."

Chief Cooper rose and went over to the kitchen window. He blew his nose—the resonant A-flat he produced on the rare occasions when emotions got the better of him. For a moment Chief Cooper stared out the window at Shellfish Bay. Then he turned back to Miguel.

"The sea skiff never crossed my mind. Not once."

~~~

The fire snapped and crackled in the stove. The twins thought about "Discussing" the misleading float plans with their father. Sara thought about Jon teetering on *Loon*'s bench, waiting to be shot. She looked up to find Jon looking anxiously at *her*. She tried to smile.

"By the way." Everyone turned to Chief Cooper. "The de Parques and the insurance people have both done a complete inventory. The treasure has been recovered, right down to the last coin and jewel. Unbelievable."

Sara's sad eyes strayed to Miguel's bandaged foot.

"Have you any idea what the recovered treasure means to you four?"

The four friends looked at each other, then at the chief.

"What does it mean?" Jon asked at last.

"It means," the chief said delicately, "that you four get a double reward: both the money from the insurance company and the reward put up by the de Parques. Not only did you have information leading to the recovery of the treasure, you recovered all of it yourselves. With a little help from Cap'n Ben, of course. And the Coast Guard."

Sara's tears had dried. She looked at her mother. "We didn't know about the rewards," she said. "That's not why we did it."

~~~

After a few more single- and two-family discussions, the Selphs and the Coopers agreed that the four friends would not be barred from their beloved boats—now, alas, a solitary boat—so long as they exercised good judgment and told the truth—all of it—in their float plans.

"Half the truth is the same as a lie," Marie Selph told them, "when you are trying to mislead someone."

"The important thing," Commander Selph told the four, "is never *ever* get into a situation you might not be able to get out of. And that means looking at consequences before you make a move, no matter how badly you want to do something. I know I keep saying that, but maybe you see why now."

"I feel awful," said a teary Sara.

"We know you do. We'd be worried if you didn't. You've learned some hard lessons and you've got some important things to think about. So do we. In time we'll all feel better. Facing up to responsibilities is always best. And your mother's right. You are four brave kids."

"Pretty smart, too." Marie Selph smiled at her tall daughter. Then she kissed Sara's moist cheek.

~~~

Ten days after their return in *Loon,* Miguel was crutching about the house. Pretty soon the big bandages would come off and the stitches would come out. When he felt the foot was ready, Miguel could try to squeeze it into a shoe.

"When you can do *that*, Miguel, you'll be pretty well healed," Doc Skillings told his patient. Then he thought for moment.

"You know, this is quite a moment for me. Never treated shot toes before. Delivered a lamb once. But no shot toes. My long medical career on Great Whale ends with distinction. Shot toes. Ay-yup."

Looking Ahead

Late Morning, Saturday, September 16

Just before noon the two families walked down *Manitou's* finger pier, Miguel crutching far ahead of the others.

A squally wind had backed into the southeast. Ragged clouds brushed the masts of the larger vessels. Over at the Coast Guard Station, the watch was hoisting the two orange pennants that signal a gale warning.

A winter sky, Sara thought. Her eyes followed a solitary white gull soaring westward on the gusty wind.

~~~

Cap'n Ben was standing on *Manitou's* dock beside a large object covered with an old sail. "Don't like to do this." He pulled the sail aside. Sara gasped.

"We sailed over to Porpoise the other day. Went right in to the cove, anchored bow and stern, and la'nched the peapod. They'd filled *Phoenix* so full of rocks we clean missed her the first time. Horace finally spotted her 'bout a fathom down over on the north side of that cove."

A large hole had been chopped in *Phoenix's* bottom, and the forward side of the outboard well had been knocked in—"Probably with one a' them fire axes, the kind with a pick on one side," Horace opined.

"The engine!" Miguel cried. "Where's the engine?"

The compass and the ensign and its staff were also gone. The rudder had been ripped off the transom and was lying inside the dory. One locker cover was hanging by a hinge. Some of the ribs and planks had been smashed. Gravel, sand, and small rocks littered the cracked and splintered floorboards.

"Those vermin! *Vermin!* I wish I'd—" Alan Selph stopped himself and walked to the end of the dock to look toward Gull Island. Jon went to stand beside the dejected Miguel.

Abbie put her arm around Sara. Marie Selph's dark eyes were brimming with tears.

"Thought twice about bringing her back looking like this—might have been better to let her lie there in peace. But if this isn't evidence, I don't know what is. State police already took their pictures. Besides. Didn't seem right not to tell Sara'n Miguel what happened to their little dory."

He and Horace passed the old sail back over *Phoenix*'s battered hull and lashed it in place against the rising wind.

"She's going to be put right," Cap'n Ben said. "Already talked with the boys over at the ship ya'd. They been over to see her. Now, Sara, you stop that." Cap'n Ben made a noise that sounded like "Hrrmph." Then he said, "Get along up that brow, Miguel. Albert's got chow ready."

~~~

Miguel hopped up *Manitou*'s accommodation ladder into her wide cockpit. From there he hopped into the doghouse and Horace lowered him down the main companion to a waiting Albert. The Selphs and Coopers clambered after him.

Jon came below last. As he turned at the bottom of the ladder, he felt once again what he always felt aboard *Manitou*: the cozy sense of being safe at home. Aromas of something delicious on the galley range and of freshly baked corn bread in the galley oven filled *Manitou*'s main saloon. The folding gimbaled table had been opened and spread with gingham place mats and napkins and bone-handled flatware. The saloon's varnished woodwork and spotless white overhead gleamed in the yellow light of the oil lamps that drove out the chilly gray day.

Jon glanced at the large aneroid barometer mounted next to a brass ship's clock on the forward port bulkhead. Pressure was dropping.

On the opposite bulkhead three bookshelves held the various publications a large sailing vessel needed if she ranged from the Caribbean to the Maritime Provinces: the Nautical Almanac, tide tables, sight reduction tables for celestial navigation, various coastal pilots, and technical manuals. Battens running the width of each shelf held the books in place.

Forward of the saloon Jon could see Albert stirring something in the stainless steel galley. Forward of the galley, Jon knew, lay the crew's quarters, but he had never been invited there.

The ship's clock chimed eight bells—*Ting-ting. Ting-ting. Ting-ting. Ting-ting.*

"Chow's ready, Cap'n," Albert called from the galley.

The two families took their seats on the settee that ran around the table and Albert ladled out the fish chowder. "There ya go, Miguel," he said. "Wrap yourself around that chowda. Good for shot toes."

Miguel grinned. "Thanks, Albert."

Albert helped the others, then sat at the forward end of the saloon table so that he could reach the galley. Everyone began to eat.

The talk in the cozy saloon was general—compliments to Albert for the chowder and the corn bread; indignation at the senseless damage to poor *Phoenix*; conjecture about the thieves' trial and the part the four friends would play as witnesses; plans to help the ya'd rebuild *Phoenix*; plans for next summer.

During a lull in the conversation, Cap'n Ben spoke up. "This might be as good a time to tell you as any," he said. "Kinda sad moment for me and Horace. This is goin' to be Albert's last winter aboard."

The others looked at the old seaman. "Ayup," said Albert. He shook his head. "Sorry to leave *Manitou* . . ."

"What are you going to do, Albert?" Jon asked respectfully.

"Retire," Albert replied. "Gettin' on, you know. Time to swallow the hook. I'll stay down in the islands when *Manitou* comes north."

Jon tried to look suitably sorrowful, but his face must have revealed what he was thinking. Cap'n Ben eyed him. "Anything on your mind, Jon?"

"Oh," Jon said off-handedly. "Oh. I don't know . . ."

"Well, I know," Cap'n Ben said decisively. Betty Cooper laughed.

"Talk it over with your folks, Jon. I've already had a word with them. Then write me in the Islands. Your mother's got the address. *Manitou's* going to need a second mate next summer. Albert and I already figured out who it ought to be . . . ''

Jon felt his ears burning. "Me?" he asked. "*Me?*"

Sara laughed delightedly. "Jonno, you should see your face!"

"Albert said he'd leave you his recipes," Cap'n Ben remarked.

Then he reached for the corn bread.

Loose Ends

The *Thresher* Gang

With Craven and Packy handcuffed below and guarded by a sailor carrying a shotgun, *Schoodic* stopped briefly in Old Town to refuel. One of Great Whale's two state troopers came aboard to take custody of Craven and Packy. Commander Selph went ashore.

Her tanks topped up, *Schoodic* sailed directly to Gardiners Port where the trooper turned Craven and Packy over to the state police waiting for them. Turco and Orcutt were already under guard at Mercy Hospital, Turco with a broken jaw and Orcutt with a fractured sternum and three cracked ribs.

Craven and Packy joined them there. Packy was in the most need of medical attention. He had been extensively burned, cut, and bruised when he was felled by the severed mast. He had suffered further when he was unceremoniously manhandled from the wheelhouse to *Thresher's* after deck.

Craven's injuries were not as serious. He had sustained a broken rib when the startled boatswain's mate had jammed him against the chain locker doorway's knife-edge. He had also received painful—but not life-threatening—bruises from the kicks the same worthy had administered to his nether regions with size-thirteen boondockers.

Thresher

The black boat was impounded by the state police and towed to Gardiners Port by a commercial tug. Forensic examiners went over every inch of her, especially the cabin where Sara and Miguel had been imprisoned.

The examiners' fingerprint results and photographs went immediately to the district attorney's office. The state's prosecutors could now prove beyond any doubt that the Selph kids had indeed been imprisoned aboard *Thresher*. The prosecutors also had the key to the cabin door, which Abbie had brought with her the night of the escape.

Legal Action

In October the four friends and their mothers traveled to Gardners Port by ferry with Great Whale Island's one attorney, old Mr. Poole. They put up at the Home Port Inn, a rare treat for islanders. The four friends were separately "deposed" over two days by lawyers from the district attorney's office in the presence of court stenographers. In effect, they were led through their stories once again through a series of well-designed questions posed by the state's prosecutors. They each then signed their depositions. Their signatures were witnessed by court employees who had not attended the depositions.

In November a grand jury indicted the four thieves on every one of the charges specified in their arraignment just after Labor Day. The four had already been assigned lawyers from the public defender's office. As of the time they were indicted, none of the four had cooperated with the state's investigation. A trial date was set for the following May.

In January little Turco, speaking thickly, agreed to plead guilty and provide evidence against Craven, Orcutt, and Packy in return for what he hoped would be a reduced sentence.

Just before the trial date in early May, the other three pled guilty to all charges, probably on the advice of their public defenders. It would have been impossible for the lawyers to challenge the evidence in the four friends' depositions and in Turco's testimony.

Turco was sentenced to twenty years in jail. Craven, Orcutt, and Packy (now a shadow of his former bulbous self) got fifty years to life.

The de Parque Treasure

Chauncey de Parque, a wealthy man by birth, inherited some of his collection of coins, jewels, and priceless artifacts and acquired the rest in his travels between the two wars. The golden crucifix may well have come from a pirate treasure hoard, though how de Parque acquired it has never been clear.

Both in their eighties and without family, the de Parques had arranged to give their priceless collection to the Boston Museum of Antiquities. The two parties were in the process of transferring owner-ship of the collection when the *Thresher* gang struck.

The thieves' timing was accidental. They knew they were hit-ting the home of a wealthy elderly couple, but they hadn't the faint-est idea there was anything special in the unprotected house. Turco apparently stumbled across the two sacks of valuables in an unlocked hall closet and made off with them. Because the two sacks were so heavy, Turco had to make two trips between the de Parque house and the sea skiff.

Miguel

Miguel was free of his crutches by Halloween and had managed to insert his foot in a shoe—*reasonably* comfortably—by winter vacation. He was playing baseball by spring and wondering if he would want to play soc-cer come fall. By May Miguel had yet to try kicking his soccer ball with his left foot.

Phoenix and *Loon*

Loon's thunderous collision with the sea skiff had cracked her port sheer strake and gunwale. Both had to be replaced after she was hauled for the winter.

Phoenix was indeed "put right," though it took the boys at the ya'd most of the winter, working on her during light spells when there wasn't too much else in hand.

Phoenix was "la'nched," as Great Whale Islanders say, on July 4, 1951. A large crowd of islanders and summer people were on hand to cheer (with all the boats in the harbor sounding their horns) as the freshly painted little green dory, with bunting over her bows and a big American flag on a new flagstaff at her stern, carried Miguel, Sara, and Abbie down the marine railway. Jon was not with his friends; *Manitou* had already departed on her first summer charter.

As *Phoenix* floated free of her cradle, Miguel started her brand-new outboard. (Just to be sure the new engine *would* start, the boys at the ya'd had mounted it on a fifty-gallon drum filled with water so that Miguel could practice this crucial procedure). Then the re-risen *Phoenix* took her place at the head of Old Town's annual Fourth of July boat parade.

Hunting for Treasure

The four friends and their parents turned down all requests for interviews and "guest appearances" on the mainland before the new-fangled "television" cameras. (There were as yet no television sets on Great Whale Island. The TV signals of 1950 could not reach that far out to sea—and a good thing, some Great Whale islanders thought.)

The Selphs and the Coopers decided, as families, that the best way to kill the inevitable rumors was for the four friends to write up the narrative of their adventures. Maybe they could get it published by the island's weekly paper, the *Mercury* (established 1841 and named for one of Old Town's early-nineteenth-century whale ships).

In January the four friends and their parents took their idea to Ephraim Beetle, editor of the *Mercury.* Knowing a sensational scoop when he saw one, the crusty old newspaperman agreed—remarkably quickly for him.

Over the winter Sara wrote the basic narrative while all four friends labored over first-person descriptions of crucial episodes in the saga. Sara wrote a slow-paced, vivid description of *Phoenix*'s first foray into the Graveyard. Abbie's account of exploring Quarantine Island with Cap'n Ben was chillingly suspenseful. Sara's narrative of the sea skiff's gunpoint capture of *Phoenix* and Capt. Craven's threats was so frightening Marie Selph went all over faint the first time she read it. Jon's and Miguel's accounts of the Battle with the Sea Skiff were understated, even matter-of-fact, and therefore the more dramatic.

Indeed, when Frances Pease, Cap'n Ben's sister and managing editor of the *Mercury,* read Jon's account of teetering on Loon's port bench while staring at the wicked pistol in Turco's hand; then when she read Miguel's description of felling Orcutt with the lead and, on top of that, kicking Turco's gun into his face as he was shot in the foot; Miss Pease dropped her blue pencil. For the first time in her editorial career, Miss Pease, who had a very sharp eye for diction, decided she would not, *could* not, change a word someone else had written.

"And they're just *kids*," she said to her brother that evening. "Just *kids*."

"Ay-yup," Ben replied. "But special."

"Not bad writers either," Miss Pease said, her highest accolade for someone else's writing.

"Ay-yup."

As *Hunting for Treasure* took shape over the winter and early spring, the four friends had known that publication would have to wait until after the trial. When Turco turned witness, however, and the other three pled guilty, all bars to the four friends' speaking about their adventures vanished.

Hunting for Treasure was published in a bound collector's edition of the *Mercury* dated July 4, 1951, the same day the newly risen *Phoenix* was launched. The initial run of five thousand copies vanished in two days. The second run flew off the shelves almost as fast, so a third run was printed.

AUTHOR'S NOTE

The models for Great Whale Island, the Little Whale Islands, and Whale Sound are, of course, Martha's Vineyard, the Elizabeth Islands, and Vineyard Sound. To justify the time of sunset on Labor Day—about 7 P.M.—I have placed the fictional islands a little north of 43° North latitude.

Some of the boats in this story are modeled on boats I knew when I was about the Cooper twins' and Sara Selph's age. I hope the boats will not mind my invoking them, particularly the real dory I knew when I was a teenager. She is the model for *Phoenix*. None of my human characters are intended to resemble anyone living or dead.

My debt to Arthur Ransome's much-loved *Swallows and Amazons* will be obvious to his devoted readers. I am equally indebted to Erskine Childers, not only for the title of my story, but for the spirit of seagoing detective work and intrepid seamanship that infuses his immortal *The Riddle of the Sands*.

I thank Lucy and Charlie Moore, my younger grandchildren, for telling me how the manuscript "read" from their perspective. I am deeply grateful to my friend Tom Dunlop, actor, journalist, and author, for reading the manuscript and encouraging me to think of publishing it.

I am equally grateful to my daughters, Louisa Hufstader and Elizabeth Balay, for helping me edit the manuscript and seeing to the myriad details necessary to prepare it for publication.

To Jan Pogue, my deep and sincere thanks. Her extensive publishing expertise was indispensable to bringing *The Riddle of the Graveyard* into print.

Finally, my family and I extend our profound thanks to John Fisher and Jennifer Caldwell. Their encouragement and financial support has made it possible for *The Riddle of the Graveyard* to reach a much wider audience than we could have reached on our own.

Peter Hufstader
Avon, Connecticut
2018

Glossary

Abaft

The sailing word for "behind," as in "the wheelhouse was located abaft [behind] the mainmast" or "the buoy appeared just abaft our beam." To be distinguished from "astern," which also means behind, as in "*Phoenix* followed ten yards astern of *Loon*."

Abeam

At right angles to, as in "We're abeam West Head light."

Anchor chain

Anchor lines made of rope in small boats like *Loon* are conventionally made fast to a galvanized chain roughly fifteen feet in length, which is in turn shackled to the anchor itself. The chain, which is much heavier than the anchor line, acts as a shock absorber when the boat is anchored, damping the boat's attempt to jerk the anchor out of the bottom as the sea rises and falls. Larger vessels like *Manitou* and *Thresher* use all-chain ground tackle.

Beam

Beam seas refers to waves coming at *Loon*'s side, rather than at her stern or bow.

"Beam" in other contexts means a boat's width at her widest point ("her beam was ten feet").

Beat, beat to windward

Sailboats cannot sail directly into the wind. When the wind was "on her nose," the gaff-rigged *Loon* had to sail at an angle of approximately 45° to the true wind, which meant a zigzag course to her destination, first on one tack, then on the other. See **Tack** below for more on points of sailing.

Boatsteerer

Aboard New England whalers, the seamen who harpooned whales were called "boatsteerers." The boatsteerer pulled the oar farthest forward in his whaleboat while one of the mates steered. When the whaleboat was within striking distance, the boatsteerer would stand and drive his harpoon (also called "iron") into the whale.

Then, as the line whizzed out of its tubs, the boatsteerer would scramble aft to steer while the mate scrambled forward to replace him in the whaleboat's bows. After this eccentric maneuver had been completed, and if the crew managed to pull the whaleboat up to the whale, the mate would kill the whale (if all went well) with a lance driven into the whale's heart, or as close to it as the mate could manage.

Break, broke

A spinnaker "breaks" when it is trimmed too far aft for the boat's angle to the wind. Instead of filling the spinnaker, the wind blows against its lee or back side, collapsing the sail, generally with a good deal of noise. If the sail is not trimmed immediately, it will continue to "flog" noisily, emitting loud *claps*.

Broad on the . . .

At a wide angle to, as in "buoy broad on the starboard bow." The opposite of "broad" is "fine," meaning at a very narrow angle to ("buoy fine on the starboard bow").

Bulwarks

Planking or steel siding rising above a vessel's main deck to keep sea water from washing people and objects over the side.

Buoys

Buoys come in different shapes, colors, and sizes. Unlighted conical red buoys are often called "nuns" because their shape supposedly resembles the silhouette of an old-fashioned nun's habit. Red buoys are even-numbered.

Odd-numbered buoys, painted green today, were painted black in 1950. These buoys are called "cans" because of their shape.

When *entering* a harbor or channel, vessels leave red buoys to starboard, the black ones to port. They do the opposite when *leaving* a harbor or proceeding toward the sea.

Red and black buoys can carry **bells** or **gongs**. A bell buoy like R "2" has only one bell struck by clappers mounted around it. A gong buoy, by contrast, carries an array of gongs with different pitches, each struck by a different clapper when the buoy moves in the sea. Other buoys make a ghastly, breathy, whistling noise as the buoy's rise and fall in a seaway forces air through a reed device. These buoys are aptly nicknamed "**groaners**." The different sounds made by gong, bell, or groaner buoys are immediately apparent to a seaman.

Buoys can display many different **light signals** to help a navigator. Some lights are fixed or steady. Others "occult": their glow begins faintly, then increases in intensity, then fades again. Some flash, either singly or in groups, sometimes quickly, sometimes at a slower pace. A lighted buoy's characteristics are always indicated on a chart. To take a real example: the buoy south of Brenton Point at the inner entrance to Narragansett Bay in Rhode Island is labeled, on the chart, "R '2' Q R WHIS," meaning it is red, it carries the white numeral "2" on its side, its red light flashes quickly and continuously, and it is a groaner ("WHIS"), not a bell or gong.

Burton tackle

More properly called a "burton." A system of blocks and lines ending in a hook, usually suspended from the forward side of a ship's mast; used when some extra power was needed to hoist something heavy or to tighten rigging.

Chain locker

A below-deck compartment aboard a larger vessel, like *Manitou* or *Thresher*, where the vessel's anchor chain would be stowed until needed.

Cheek Block

A wooden case into which sheaves are fitted. "This image shows a sheave inside wooden cheeks. The sheave would turn as the rope or line ran through the block, reducing friction and keeping the line from chafing.

Cleat

A wooden or metallic device with protruding horns used for securing or "belaying" lines. The action of securing a line around a cleat is called "cleating." "The line pictured here is correctly cleated. The finishing half hitch lies parallel to the rest of the line's turns around the cleat's horns.

Close Reach

A point of sailing somewhere between a beam reach (the wind at an angle of 90° to the boat's course) and close-hauled (the boat is sailing as close to the wind as she can efficiently). See **Tack** below for more on points of sailing.

Coaming

A lip of wood about three inches high that runs around a sailboat's cockpit to keep water from running into the cockpit and thence into the bilge. See Jon's schematic drawing of *Loon* on p. 104.

Comber

A long, curling wave that builds up near a shoreline—the kind surfers love.

Compass

The illustration below shows a magnetic compass marked off in the old-fashioned point system that has pretty much vanished. Most compasses today are marked off in degrees alone, making them more accurate to steer by and much easier to read.

Phoenix's **box compass** was pretty much what the name implies: a compass inside a protective box like the one shown below. Both *Loon* and *Phoenix* had little square brackets made out of quarter-round moldings so placed (*Phoenix*'s on the midships thwart, *Loon*'s on her cockpit sole) that when the compass was sitting in the bracket, its "lubber line" was lined up with the bow of the boat, which would help the helmsman keep her on an accurate course.

Compass rose

A diagram of a compass printed on a chart in exact alignment with the true and magnetic north poles. The compass rose helped Jon plot his approximate bearings as *Phoenix* traveled toward Sei Island. "The compass rose on *Phoenix*'s chart would have looked very much like the compass rose printed on the chart pictured under Dividers on p. 170.

Current and tide

"Current" refers to the lateral flow of water between low water and high water and back to low again. Knowing the direction and strength of current is crucial to safe and efficient navigation, as the four friends' adventures illustrate.

"Tide" refers to the rise and fall of the sea as it moves between low water and high water, also called low and high tide. The tide goes from high to low and back again to high roughly every six hours. The times of high and low tide are contained in many reference volumes, some published by the government and some published privately.

Current and tides are controlled by the moon as it passes in its elliptical orbit around the earth.

When the tide is rising in Whale Sound, the current moves from southwest to northeast. When the tide falls, the current moves from northeast to southwest.

When the tide is rising, currents in the Graveyard, Butler's Hole, and the narrow "gutters" threading the Little Whale Island move *from* Butler's Bay into Whale Sound and thence toward the east. They move in the opposite direction when the tide is falling.

Deadlight

A piece of glass or other transparent material fixed in a door or a bulkhead to admit light. Deadlights cannot be opened so they do not provide ventilation.

Dividers

A two-legged navigation instrument (on the lower right-hand corner) rather like the compass used in geometry class. Navigators use dividers to measure distances on a chart.

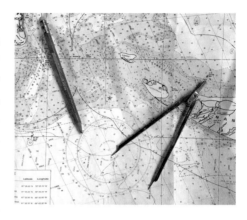

Dory

Dories were small, flat-bottomed boats carried in nests by Grand Banks schooners from which cod and halibut were caught by long trawl lines. *Phoenix* was modeled after Grand Banks dories.

Eight bells

In this case (p. 155), noon. Bells chiming every half hour count out each four-hour "watch," or duty period, aboard a vessel. The bell system begins with one bell at 12:30, 4:30, 8:30, and 12:30 again, two bells on the next hour, and so on, right around the clock, night and day, with odd numbered bells on the half hour, even on the hour.

The watches themselves are named the **first watch** (8 p.m. to midnight; **middle watch** (midnight to 4 a.m.; **morning watch** (4 a.m. to 8 a.m.); **forenoon watch** (8 a.m. to noon); and **afternoon watch** (noon to 4 p.m.). The next four-hour watch is divided into "dog" watches, the "**first dog**" going from 4 p.m. to 6 p.m. and the "**second dog**" from 6 p.m. to 8 p.m., done so that the crew is spared from repeating the same watches every day. Then at 8 p.m. the first watch begins and the system continues as described above.

Engine well

An engine well is basically a hole cut in a boat's bottom and surrounded by bulwarks on all four sides to keep the water in its proper place. The dory's engine is mounted on the forward bulkhead of the well. "The engine well pictured here is elongated to allow the engine to be tilted forward, thereby lifting its propeller off the bottom when the boat is beached. This is what Miguel does when the captured *Phoenix* is forced at gunpoint onto the rocky beach at Porpoise Island.

Fathom

A nautical term for six feet. Depth of water can be indicated on charts in fathoms, feet, or meters, which is why we must always check our charts' legends to learn how they indicate soundings. It is very important to know whether that "2" on the chart means feet or fathoms or meters.

Fenders

Cylindrical shapes made of soft, compressible material hung over a boat's side to protect it from being damaged by a dock or another boat.

Fisherman's anchor

Manitou's fisherman's anchor was the same design as but bigger and more rugged than this one.

Flank speed

The fastest speed a Coast Guard vessel can make. Flank speed uses a great deal of fuel.

Foreguy

A line keeping the spinnaker pole from "skying" up past the horizontal, which it wants to do in any kind of breeze. The foreguy leads from the end of the pole to a turning block on the foredeck and then aft to the cockpit where it is secured.

Foul Ground

An area where rocks, wreckage, or other obstacles may make it difficult to anchor.

Gaff Rig

A plan of *Loon*'s gaff rig appears on p. 104. The throat halyard hoists the inboard end of the gaff. The peak halyard hoists the outboard end of the gaff. Both halyards are hoisted together, the gaff traveling upward horizontally until the block on the throat hits its mate on the mast. Then the throat halyard is cleated and the peak halyard is hoisted until the peak is also all the way up, as in this image.

Gunwale

Pronounced "GUH-nl." The top edge of an open boat's sides.

Guy

The control line attached to the spinnaker pole.

Harden up

To alter course toward the wind. Altering course away from the wind is called "heading off," "bearing off," or "falling off."

Heading us

On p. 122, the wind is shifting from the northwest to the north, which makes it blow more over *Loon*'s bow than over her side. The wind's new angle of attack makes it difficult for *Loon* to carry her spinnaker. To compensate for the shift, Jon tells Abbie to "head off," meaning to starboard, to bring the wind back on *Loon*'s beam again. That would make the spinnaker break less but it would also turn *Loon* away from her direct course home. But Jon reassures Abbie that the flooding current, moving from the southwest to the northeast, will "set" *Loon* back on her course *to* West Head though she is not pointing directly *at* West Head.

Jibe

Turning a boat running before the wind so that its stern passes through the wind. As the stern passes through the wind, the main boom swings over to the other side and the boat is now on the other tack, or jibe. See the Tack diagram p. 175 for the different points of sail.

Mainsheet

The control line for the mainsail, which is attached to the main boom. See Jon's sail plan for *Loon* on p. 104.

Mast hoops

Wooden hoops encircling the mast to which the luff (leading edge) of the mainsail is attached. Mast hoops hold the luff close to the mast as the gaff is hoisted or lowered. Sometimes called parrels. See the drawing of *Loon* on p. 104.

Monkey's fist

A large, heavy knot used to weight the end of a heaving line so deck hands can throw the line from a ship to waiting dockhands. Monkey's fists were often knotted around lead weights to make them even heavier. The heaving line was a thin line attached to the much heavier hawser, which would secure the ship to the dock. Since it would be impossible to throw the hawser, the monkey's fist was thrown first, pulling the heaving line after it. The dockhands would then pull the heaving line in and the hawser would follow.

Mushroom anchor

An anchor with a mushroom-shaped bottom instead of flukes generally used for moorings.

New Moon

The moon's dark phase, when the moon is on the same side of the earth as the sun. A new moon sheds no light on earth because the sun is shining on the side away from our planet. The converse is true when the moon is full. Since it is on the opposite side of the earth from the sun, the sun illuminates it fully.

Painter

Rover's bowline, which secured the battered little dinghy to its mushroom anchor.

Perigee

The point at which the moon is closest to the earth in its elliptical orbit around the planet. Tides are highest and lowest and currents run strongest when a full or new moon occurs at perigee. The opposite of perigee is apogee, the point where the moon is farthest from the earth and where its influence on tides and currents is least.

Port and Starboard

Nautical names for left and right.

Quahog

The Atlantic clam. On Great Whale Island, quahog is pronounced "KO-hog."

Rigger's Knife

A stout knife with a broad, blunt-headed blade used for cutting line and rope. The rigger's knife also has a sharp, tapered marlin spike used to separate the strands of laid rope when splicing and doing other rigging tasks that require a pointed device that won't cut what it penetrates.

Sheaves

Flanged metal wheels or pulleys fitted inside turning blocks to allow lines to pass through blocks with the least amount of friction. You can see sheave inside the wooden cheek block pictured on page 167.

Sheer Strake

The topmost, therefore longest, plank on a boat's side above the waterline

Sheet

A line used to control a sail, as in jib sheet and main sheet.

Sound

A body of water lying between land masses and open at either end, as with Whale Sound. A bay, by contrast, has no exit. You must leave a bay by the way you came in.

Spinnaker

A large, full-bellied sail used off the wind to increase a sailboat's speed. This image shows Marconi-rigged sloops (*Loon* was gaff rigged) with spinnakers set.

Spring Lines

Docking lines that prevent a vessel from moving forward or astern in her berth.

Spudge barrel

The origin of this name for the bait barrel aboard a lobster boat is obscure. I picked it up from a friend who said he first heard it from a Maine lobsterman.

Steadying sails

Some power vessels use small steadying sails in beam winds and seas to reduce rolling. Pressure against the steadying sail from a beam wind keeps the power boat heeled to leeward, as if she were a sailing vessel. Without a steadying sail, the high-profile power boat would roll uncomfortably from side to side in beam winds and seas.

Starboard ten

Ten degrees to the right (or to starboard) of the ship's course.

Steep-to shore

A shoreline where the water remains relatively deep until quite near the beach, allowing a keel boat like *Loon* to anchor very close to shore.

Steerage way

Sailboats' rudders don't work unless there is water moving by them. That means that a sailboat must always be moving if she is to be steered. That movement is called steerage way.

Sternway

A boat's backward movement through the water.

Swallow the hook

"Hook" is sailing slang for "anchor." When Albert says he's going to "swallow the hook" down in the islands, he means he is going to retire, or "anchor himself" permanently ashore.

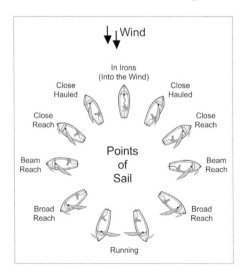

Tack

The noun "tack" refers to the angle of the wind to the boat. When the wind is blowing across the boat's starboard side and her main boom is to port, she is on the starboard tack, as in the image to the left.

The verb "tack" refers to the maneuver of bringing the boat's bow through the wind from one tack onto the other tack, as from the starboard tack onto the port tack. The boat close-hauled on the starboard tack at the top of the diagram below is shown tacking through the wind onto the port tack.

The maneuver called "jibing" or "jibe," defined in a separate entry above, is the opposite of tacking. In a jibe, the stern of the right-hand "running" boat at the bottom of the diagram above moves through the eye of the wind. When this happens, the boom bangs from the starboard side across to the port side. The boat is then on the starboard tack.

The diagram also lists the names of the other points of sailing and shows a boat's angle to the wind when on each point of sailing.

The term "in irons" just under the wind arrows at the top of the diagram refers to a situation no competent sailor *ever* wants to get into (but most, to their embarrassment, have). When a boat attempting to tack lacks enough steerage way to cross through the eye of the wind onto the other tack, she stops dead, loses steerage, and begins to gather sternway. The best way to recover is to allow the boat to gather speed astern until she recovers her steerage way. Then you put the helm over in the direction you want the bow to go—steering astern is exactly the opposite of steering going ahead— and steer the boat's bow around to the other tack, at which point her sails will fill and she will gain forward momentum.

Thimble

A tear-drop-shaped fitting with flanges made of galvanized metal, aluminum, or heavy plastic. An anchor line is spliced around the thimble, which is then secured to an anchor chain. The thimble prevents the anchor line from being chafed by the chain.

This image shows a wire cable passed around a metal thimble.

Tiller lines

Tiller lines are attached to a yoke mounted on the head of a rudder. When Sara was steering *Phoenix*, a pull on the port line (the left one) turned the dory to port; a pull on the starboard line turned *Phoenix* to starboard.

Transom

The deck of a sailboat abaft the cockpit. See the diagram of *Loon* on p. 104. During *Loon*'s battle with the sea skiff, Jon stood on her transom, his left foot braced against one of the sloop's mainsheet blocks.

Way, losing way

Way is the nautical term for a boat's momentum. Large, deep-keeled vessels like *Manitou* can "carry their way," or maintain their momentum, for a very long distance after their sails are taken down (doused). When *Manitou* approaches Quarantine Island, it takes three full 360° turns after the sails are doused before *Manitou* loses enough way for Cap'n Ben to order the anchor lowered.

Weather side

The windward side of the boat, or the side closer to the wind. The opposite of **weather** is **leeward**, the side away from the wind.